"Dreams Do Come True"

A Lesbian Romance

Jenny Bloom

© 2020
Jenny Bloom

All rights reserved. No part of this publication may be reproduced, distributed, or transmitted in any form or by any means, including photocopying, recording, or other electronic or mechanical methods, without the prior written permission of the publisher, except in the case of brief quotations embodied in critical reviews and certain other non-commercial uses permitted by copyright law.

This book is intended for Adults (ages 18+) only. The contents may be offensive to some readers. It may contain graphic language, explicit sexual content, and adult situations. May contain scenes of unprotected sex. Please do not read this book if you are offended by content as mentioned above or if you are under the age of 18. Please educate yourself on safe sex practices before making potentially life-changing decisions about sex in real life.

This story is a work of fiction. Names, characters, businesses, places, events and incidents are the products of the author's imagination or used in a fictitious manner & are not to be construed as real. Any resemblance to actual persons, living or dead, or actual events is purely coincidental. Products or brand names mentioned are trademarks of their respective holders or companies. The cover uses licensed images & are shown for illustrative purposes only. Any person(s) that may be depicted on the cover are simply models.

Edition v1.00 (2020.02.04)
www.JennyBloomAuthor.com

Special thanks to the following volunteer readers who helped with proofreading: Jenny, Naomi W., RB and those who assisted but wished to be anonymous. Thank you so much for your support.

Chapter One

Alicia walked over to the counter, taking the next customer in line. Working at this store wasn't always the most fun, but it was a decent job, paid more than minimum wage, and it wasn't working at Amazon, so she wasn't going to complain.

"All right, your total is $20.61."

"I thought that was on sale," the lady said.

"Ma'am, your coupon is expired," Alicia said.

"Of course, you damn kids are all like this. I'm very unsurprised," she uttered.

"Excuse me, could you not act like that toward my employees," a voice said.

Alicia turned, seeing her best friend, Melanie. She stood there, her blonde hair tied back in a pony, looking at the belligerent woman with annoyance on her face.

"But—"

"Your coupon doesn't work. I'm sorry, I'm not going to fulfill it. You should know better. I will suggest that you do take the current discount that's going on. You're still paying less than normal," she stated.

"Hmph, like you'd understand. You kids are all the same," she muttered.

"Would you like me to check you out?" Melanie asked.

"All right. It's okay. The cashier is on her phone anyway. You should look at the employees that you have," she said to Melanie.

Alicia looked at her with shock in her eyes. She was only on her phone for a second, waiting for the woman to finish! Alicia looked at Melanie, noticing that she was sighing.

"I'm sorry, ma'am. Now, let's finish the transaction, and I'll let you go on your merry way," Melanie said.

"Fine," she muttered.

As Alicia watched Melanie finish up, she felt anger, but at the same time, she was relieved that Melanie offered to help out. The rest of the customers were taken care of, and Alicia sighed. She wanted to scream, especially since she was treated so crappy by the people today.

"The Christmas season can go suck it. Why is everyone so shitty to everyone," she lamented.

"I know Alicia. But, if that happens again, please be cordial. I know how annoying people can be, but please be smart with your actions," Melanie forewarned.

Alicia sighed. "You're right. These old fucks are all like that, but I guess that's par for the course. It's better than trying to find a job in this Market anyways," Alicia said.

"I know how people can be. Trust me, being the manager here isn't easy. But you've done so good, and I'm so happy to have you on my team," she said with a purr.

When Melanie smiled at Alicia, she looked directly at Melanie with widened eyes. Why was Melanie so perfect? Melanie was so sweet and lovely. Alicia didn't know what to do other than smile back.

"I'm trying to do my best. You are a kick-ass manager, though," Alicia said.

"Thank you. I try. I really do," Melanie said.

"Well, you do it so well. I'm always happy to work with you," Alicia said.

The truth was, Alicia took this job partially because she needed it, but also because she liked working with her best friend. Alicia had a crush on her, but she always feared pursuing it since she didn't want to make things weird. After all, they were coworkers, and it was frowned upon.

Still, she always marveled at Melanie's actions. The two of them were best friends ever since they were kids. Melanie was about two years older than Alicia, at twenty-one years old, but she already had so much going on. In truth, Alicia felt a little jealous. All she could do was draw shitty chibis and hope that she would finish her college degree sooner rather than later.

"Well, I'm glad you're here with me, Alicia. Anyway, we need to finish restocking," she said.

Alicia nodded, and the two of them continued to work together. However, Alicia's hands and Melanie's kept brushing, and every time they did, Alicia felt like her hands were on fire.

She never thought their relationship would amount to anything, since they were just friends. But she did hope that one day, she'd have the courage to spend time with Melanie, and hopefully one day, she'd make this all work.

As they finished the shift, Danny whistled.

"The place looks great," he said.

"Thanks. Nice to see you contributed," Alicia replied sardonically.

"Relax, I'm going to be here tonight. You're off early," Danny said with a smile.

"Now, now, don't fight you two," Melanie said.

Alicia immediately shut up, and Danny smiled.

"All right, fearless leader. I won't fight with her. In fact, I'm going to help Alicia out," he said.

"Thanks," Alicia said.

He was a nice guy, but Alicia didn't like Danny all that much. He was a nice guy, but just that: a nice guy who irritated her more than anything. After they finished preparing the shop for the next shift, Alicia left the store.

"Oh, Alicia!" Melanie said.

Alicia whipped her head around, noticing Melanie's face. She seemed a bit nervous.

"What's up? Something the matter?"

"No. I just wanted to ask if you wanted to go out and get some coffee after tomorrow's shift? It's a long one, and we'll have a pretty long ass day. But I was thinking that maybe just getting some coffee together after the chaos would be nice," Melanie offered.

Alicia stopped. She wondered if this was her way of asking her out on a date. She didn't think Melanie saw her like that, but she smiled.

"Sure, I'd love that, Mel," she said.

"Great. It's a date then," Melanie said with a teasing wink.

As she left, Alicia stood there, trying to process what just happened. Did she get a date? Was this even real? Alicia didn't even know anymore, but she'd take it, even though she had no idea what would happen next.

Chapter Two

Melanie felt her heart skip a beat when Alicia agreed to it.

It was the first time she asked someone out on a date like that. Alicia did like Melanie, but she always thought they'd be nothing more than friends. Life was easier that way. She never thought of pursuing something like this. When she spoke to Melanie, hearing her agree to go out, made her begin to wonder if she might be onto something.

"No, I can't be. It's not like Alicia liked me like that," Melanie muttered to herself.

While Alicia was kind, she never thought they'd become something more. After all, Melanie wasn't out of the closet, and she didn't believe that Alicia was either. She just thought that Alicia was sweet. But, maybe finally getting a grasp on her feelings might do her some good.

As she went back over to the counter, Brayden smiled.

"I can see the blush—"

"Can it. I don't like her like that," she said. That was a total lie, though.

"Relax, Melanie. I won't say anything," he said with a purr.

Melanie stopped, feeling the redness on her face grow once again.

"Anyways, I think it's best if we make it out to be some huge thing. I'm still coming to terms with this," Melanie said.

"You know, you don't have to lie to yourself there, Melanie. If you want to go on a date with her, I doubt it's a problem," Braydon said.

"I don't think Alicia is into girls," Melanie muttered.

"You'd be surprised. It's always the quiet ones who are," Braydon said.

"Alicia may be quiet, but I don't know. Maybe I'm too confident about this," Melanie admitted. She didn't know what she would do if Alicia were actually into girls.

"I mean, you've known her for years, Melanie. Has she ever said anything about finding women pretty?" Braydon said.

"Nope. I don't ever hear her talk about that. She talks about her mom, who doesn't seem to care all that much about her. And how life's been hard since her parents separated about five years back. I don't remember the details, but I think it had something to do with her husband cheating," Melanie said.

"Sheesh, that's rough," Danny said.

"Yeah. I'm just trying to be there for Alicia as best as I can. I'm not the best at it, and I know how hard it can be on her. Alicia is strong, I've been with her through the worst, and I'm not giving up on her now," Melanie said.

Melanie finished her shift. Then, after it was over, she felt a presence nearby. It was Braydon.

"You're still thinking about it, aren't you," he said.

"Why do you ask?" she muttered.

"I can see your concern there, Melanie. If you had done something wrong toward Alicia, it would've been mentioned by now. I think you're doing the right thing," he said.

Glad one of them thought so.

"I'm just worried. I mean, I doubt Alicia feels the same way. Realizing I want to be around her is strange. I don't know if it's a crush or something more," she admitted.

Melanie always felt like they'd be best friends forever. Braydon lightly touched her side, smiling.

"Well, if you ever need to talk about girl troubles, just hit me up. I'm all right with them," Braydon said.

"Yeah, because you date every girl that gives you the time of day," she muttered.

"Ouch, you're cold there, Melanie. Well, you have my support. Aren't you supposed to be getting a promotion here too?" he said.

She nodded. "Yeah. They want to make me the first assistant manager, but I'm not sure. That Danny guy is so weird, though. He's always super stiff whenever Alicia is brought up," Melanie pointed out.

"I think we all went to high school with him. He may have been one of those guys nobody associated with since he's kind of odd," he said to Melanie.

"You're telling me. Danny is always glaring at me like I did something and is a bit rude to us. So far, the little bully is covering his tracks well," she said.

"Yeah, bullies do that. We should get going. You have a little date with Alicia tomorrow," he teased.

"I told you, it's not a date," she said.

"Oh, I know. But that little outburst makes me think you didn't mean to hide your tracks," Braydon teased.

Melanie lightly slapped his shoulder.

***

Melanie went home, seeing her mom in the living room. Her dad was in his office.

Things at home were decent, unlike at Alicia's.

"Hey, Mom. Hi Dad," she said.

"Hello, dear. How was work?" Melanie's mother asked.

"Great. I'm working hard to get another promotion. I think this next one is for the first assistant manager. I'm quite happy with it," she said.

"Indeed. Do you think you'll have a corporate job there?" Melanie's dad asked.

Melanie shrugged.

"I don't know. I mean, it's different than what I'm going to college for. Not sure if it's worth it or not, but I'm still chugging along," Melanie said.

"It's a job that has good security. Might be worth staying," Melanie's mother said.

Melanie didn't know how to feel about her job. On the one hand, she was happy to have it. On the other hand, she wished she could just up and leave.

"I don't know. It's not what I want to do," Melanie said.

"Painting isn't worth leaving the field you're in, though dear. You know this," her mother snapped.

She did, but that didn't make it any less comfortable.

"I know, but still. Doesn't make life all that easy, you know," she said.

"Well, you should be mindful of what you're doing there, Melanie. You should know by now that if you're not careful, it'll end up biting you in the backside," her mother said.

"We'll help as we can, but you also need to make a name for yourself," her father admonished.

It was always this discussion. Melanie would tell her family a little bit about the job she did. Then suddenly it turned to them asking when she would get a promotion and to give up her "silly" art.

"I'm not giving up my art. I'm going to stick with it. It makes me happy. I don't care if it's a side thing, I love doing it," she said.

"Well, be smart," her mother said.

"It won't pay for your future," her father added.

Melanie always hated this discussion. They were so supportive, but they never wanted her to make art a job. She understood why, but still. She also knew that the future of her time at the company might also be affected by any sudden job changes.

She went to her room, sighing as she laid there. As much as she'd love to tell her family to knock it off, to let her live her own life, and to be happy doing her own thing, she knew better than to get into that with them. It's better just ignoring them and doing what she did best. And that, of course, was living her own life.

Still, Melanie couldn't stop thinking about the interaction she had with Alicia. The two of them were close after all these years, but Melanie feared they might be slowly drifting apart in a sense. They hadn't spent much time together, at least compared to the past. She did miss Alicia a little bit, but she thought if she did tell her about it, she might be overstepping her boundaries.

That night, Melanie worked on homework, trying her best not to get super hung up on anything that was going on. Instead, she kept herself together, worked on all of the different aspects of her projects, and made sure everything was done before the next day. It was a typical night for her in a sense, and she wondered what might transpire next, and she hoped that, no matter what happened, everything would work itself out.

Maybe things would change, but Melanie imagined if she told Alicia how she felt, she might lose Alicia in the process.

Chapter Three

Alicia dreaded heading back home, but she had to do what she had to do. When she walked through the door, she saw the house was empty.

Not like it was something she wasn't used to.

In a sense, it was almost like she was living alone most days. Her mother was never around, and she always felt like she was the one cooking food for them. She set up the pressure cooker which her mother managed to finally get after Alicia said she would pay for half and cooked some food.

"Where is she?" she muttered to herself.

Suddenly, a crash echoed through the doorway. Alicia looked up. There was her mother, the bags of groceries scattered all over the ground. She looked at Alicia with a look of pure annoyance.

"Can I get some help here?" Alicia's mother said.

"I don't know, can you," Alicia said.

"Watch your tongue. If it weren't for me, you wouldn't have food," her mother said.

"Sorry. You okay?" Alicia asked.

"Oh, just the usual. Going from job to job has been hard for me," Alicia's mother said.

"I understand that. Did you manage to find one with better hours?"

"Nope. It's going to be another weekend from hell. On top of that, I work until five all week long. The holiday season sucks, but that's how it is. I'd love for it to be easier, but ever since your dad stopped paying child support since you're an adult, it made things much rougher," she said.

"Have you spoken to him at all? I barely remember him. It's been about ten years since you guys divorced, and he hasn't made an effort to see us. I was just wondering," Alicia asked.

"Nope, and I doubt I ever will. The rat bastard forgot about both of us," she snapped.

Alicia sighed. It was always like this. Her mother would always blame her relationship issues on her dad.

"Oh yeah, by the way, I'll be gone tomorrow night. I'm meeting up with my boss, and I plan to stay out a bit late with him," she said.

Alicia looked at her mother with a narrowed glance.

"You're not going to fuck him, are you?"

Her mother scoffed.

"Why would you think I'd do that? I'm his coworker. I'm working for him. It's wrong," she said.

But, from the tone of voice alone, Alicia knew that was a total lie.

"Whatever just don't do anything too stupid, okay?" she said.

"You're one to talk. By the way, when are you bringing home a cute boy for me to meet? I'd love to see who you attract," she said.

Alicia tensed. Her mother didn't know that she was very gay and has pined for Melanie for years. She almost asked her to the high school formal but opted out and went alone because she knew it would cause problems.

"I don't... I don't do much besides work and online classes. And I mean, my animations," Alicia said.

"Oh, those stupid things. Alicia, you need to find a better job, something that fits you better," she said.

Alicia felt her blood begin to boil when she heard her mother say those words. She couldn't believe her mother thought they were just stupid animations.

"They're not stupid, Mom. I have created some cool content, and I'm excited to put it all together," she said.

"Well, it's not going to pay the bills. Besides, aren't you a little too old for that anime crap," her mother muttered.

Alicia hated it when she got like this. Her mom had a penchant for being a total dick at times for no fucking reason.

"Mom, it's not weird anime crap. Besides, I'm helping around the house, I pay the bills, and I'm happy with my job and my life. Maybe you should learn to humble yourself a tiny bit," she said.

"You watch your mouth, Alicia. You only pay for a quarter of the things around here. I'm always working. Perhaps, you should get another job if you think running your mouth like that is tolerated here," she snapped.

Alicia felt hurt the moment she heard her mother say those things. She always felt like she was getting shafted like this. But, every time she tried to fight it, her mom would always bring this up.

"It's always like this. You're always telling me how shitty of a kid I am, even though I try hard. I work on myself, and I try to make do with what's best for all of us. Maybe you should learn some respect," Alicia said.

Her mother slammed her plate down on the table, walking over and grabbing Alicia, holding her against the wall.

"Listen here, missy. If you continue to be smart with me, I'll make sure your life is a living hell. Now be a good girl, work, and find yourself a nice boy to marry. Then, I won't have to take care of you and your bullshit anymore. Got it," she said.

Alicia felt her release her hands, sighing as she took her food and went to her room. Alicia's eyes filled with tears at the realization that it would always be like this.

"Why is she always such a fucking bitch?" she said.

Alicia marched upstairs, opening the door to her bedroom and then closing it. When she got in there, she noticed all of the anime posters and small figurines she'd collected. Alicia sighed, feeling her head filled with a lot of worry and doubt.

She felt isolated in her own home. She felt like her mother would continue this until something gave. When she sat at her computer, working on her homework and then her animations, she smiled to herself.

Creating animations was what made her happy. Alicia would kill to be an animator for a company. She wanted that type of job more than anything else. She had already sent out a variety of applications, and tonight was no exception.

"I hope there's someone out there that can help me have a better life, a better time, and feel good about this," she muttered to herself.

Alicia had a lot of things eating away at her. She wondered if there was anything further to do. She certainly had her doubts and worries. However, Alicia knew it would eventually get better.

Alicia hoped her date would at least amount to something. If she could admit to Melanie she had a crush on her, she would be the happiest woman alive.

Chapter Four

Melanie was nervous. She stood at the counter, while Alicia took care of restocking shelves, counting down the minutes until she was off the clock.

"Are you okay, Melanie?" Braydon asked, bringing a box nearby.

"Yes. Sorry, I have a lot on my mind. Didn't get the best sleep the other night," she explained.

"I see. Been thinking about your little date," Braydon teased.

"Please fuck off," she replied.

Braydon laughed, and Melanie sat at the desk, sighing in annoyance. She just wanted to get the date over with and figure out if the feelings within her were real.

When it was finally time, Melanie clocked out almost immediately. She noticed that Alicia was right there with her. Melanie smiled at her, feeling excited about this.

"Are you okay?" Alicia said.

"Yes. Sorry, I was thinking about this day. It was such a long day. All of the customers I dealt with were annoying, too," Melanie admitted.

"Well, let's get out of here," Alicia said.

They walked out together. Instead of going to the coffee shop right around the corner, Alicia went toward the one across the street.

"I like this place better. A more intimate atmosphere," Alicia said.

"Either is fine with me. I'm just going into here to spend time with you anyway," Melanie admitted.

She flushed as she uttered those words, realizing that they were slightly embarrassing.

"Aww, you're sweet," Alicia said.

When they got in there, they each ordered a cup of coffee, sitting around at the table.

"You know, you never ask me out like this. We've been friends since we were kids, and you've always just said 'hey let's go shopping' and other things. Why the sudden change?" Alicia asked.

Melanie shrugged. "I don't know. I just wanted to take you somewhere a little different. You know, I'm glad that you came onto my team. I was worried you wouldn't take the job when I initially offered it," Melanie pointed out.

"Oh, trust me. I needed a job. My mom was a total asshole about it," she said.

"Like how she always is," Melanie pointed out.

Alicia's mother was a bitch, and she hated Melanie for no good reason. Melanie just wished that she could take Alicia away from her, to save her from her mother's power and effect. But Alicia sighed.

"My mom was mad that I was working with you and on my animations. I found out she got another job. She'll be gone most weekends in December, which is a good thing. I like my mom, but I always feel like she's lying to me and hasn't told me the whole story," Alicia said.

"Like about your dad?" Melanie asked.

"Yes. I've looked for information and asked her about it, but my mother won't give me anything. I feel like there's something deeper there, but I don't know what," Alicia said.

Melanie pursed her lips. "I don't know what I can do to help you, but I am going into profiling for the police department. Maybe the tools they provide me will help with this," she said.

"Right. I mean, if you ever run across anything, I'll take it. For all I know, my father could be dead," she said.

"I doubt he's dead. If your mom isn't responding, it's more likely she doesn't want you to talk to him because it'll give your ideas. I know how people can be," she said.

"Will you still be at the store after the holidays?"

"I don't know. The company wants me to work in their branch office, which is nearby. I don't know if this is the path I want to take," Melanie said.

"Why is that?"

Alicia asked.

"I don't know. I wish I could do my own thing. I don't want to get stuck in this company instead of doing what I truly want to do with my life. I seem to be preoccupied with that," she said.

Alicia nodded. "I know what you mean. I want to work in animation, but ugh, the job listings for it are few and far between. It's hard," she said.

"You're telling me. I always feel like I'm just biding my time, waiting for the right moment to strike," Melanie admitted.

"That makes two of us. But I guess it'll get easier with time," Alicia said with a smile.

"Right. So, I kind of wonder what's going to happen from here. We've always been close. Even though we're adults, we still spend our time together.

You've grown up, Alicia. You've become quite pretty," Melanie said.

Alicia felt her face heat at those words. Melanie blushed as well, shaking her head.

"I'm nothing compared to you. You are so beautiful, Melanie," she said.

Melanie tensed. Did Alicia feel the same way? That they were both awkwardly swimming around the subject.

"Thank you. You know, I sometimes wonder if things would've been easier if we had families that understood us, rather than making sure our lives are hard," she said.

"I've wondered that too. But, I'm glad that I have you, Melanie. I really am," Alicia replied.

"I'm glad as well. You've always been there for me, and I don't want to lose you either," Melanie stated.

Melanie hesitated to touch Alicia's hand and tell her that she liked her. Melanie wanted to say the words, but she didn't know what might happen.

"By the way, are you off Saturday?" Alicia asked.

"Of course. Why?"

"My mom works late on Saturday. I wondered if you wanted to go to the ice-skating rink together?" Alicia asked.

Melanie tensed. Was Alicia asking her out for another date? She wondered if this was even a date period. But she quickly nodded.

"I would love that, Alicia. I don't want to screw up what I already have with you. If you're free to go out this weekend together, I'd love that. I wouldn't mind sticking around after. Do you think your mom will be back?"

"I highly doubt it. My mom said that she's working more jobs around the holidays. I'm not sure if it's for the guys she's seeing or for me. But I don't think she'll be around. So, you're welcome to come over," Alicia replied.

"I'd love that. Let's meet up again on Saturday then," Melanie replied.

When they finished, they both got up, awkwardly brushing their hands together. They walked back over to the store. Alicia looked at Melanie for a moment. Melanie ventured to ask, wondering if there was more to the date than she thought.

"Are you okay?" she asked Alicia.

"Yes, it's just that you're holding my hand," Alicia pointed out.

Melanie quickly retracted her hand, looking at Alicia with a blush on her face.

"Oh God, I'm so sorry," she said.

"Relax, I liked it, Mel. You're too worried. It's nice to have my hand touched like that," she said.

"It is nice," Melanie said.

They held each other's hands for a moment, neither of them wanting to leave. However, Alicia then slowly moved back, looking at Melanie with a grin.

" I'll see you Saturday, right?" she asked.

"Yes. For sure. It's a date," Melanie said.

As Alicia left, Melanie then kicked herself mentally for saying it was a date again, but she wanted it to be such. It was nice to finally express her feelings, even if it was a little bit awkward to do so.

Chapter Five

As Melanie left to go back to her place, Alicia stood there, feeling nervous about how this would all play out. There were three days until Saturday. Alicia wondered if there was something else that she could do at this point.

She went back home. She noticed her mother wasn't around. But Alicia still felt a little anxious about what to do next.

She was happy things with Melanie were somewhat what she expected. But she wasn't quite able to figure out their relationship. Everything felt so weird, so different for her. Alicia wondered just what she could do about it.

***

That evening, Alicia heard her mother come in around midnight. She walked downstairs, only to find her drunk and hobbling about.

"Hello," her mother said.

"Hey, Mom. You're drunk," Alicia said.

"I'm no' drunk. I jus' had a little drink," she said.

Alicia sighed. It'd been a while since she had to deal with a drunken mom acting like a fool.

"Come on, Mom. Let's get you to bed," she said.

"No, I want to stay up," she insisted.

Alicia shook her head. Not this again. Sometimes, her mom would say fuck it and randomly get drunk. It was indeed one of those nights. Right now, Alicia wasn't having it.

"All right, come on," Alicia offered.

She grabbed her mom's hand, bringing her upstairs and to bed. As her mother fell asleep, Alicia sighed.

"Hey, Mom, I'll be hanging out with Melanie this weekend. She may come over. Is that okay?"

"Sure. As long as she doesn't touch things," her mother simply said.

Suddenly, she was out cold. Alicia wondered if it was just pure luck, or because her mom was drunk. In any case, she was just happy that she at least had some bit of an edge over her mom right now.

***

The next day, Alicia went to the store. However, she noticed a bouquet of roses in her cubby.

"Hi Melanie?" she asked as she walked outside with them.

"Hi, Alicia. Is everything all right?"

"It is. Someone left this bouquet in my cubby. I'm don't get it. I think the flowers are for someone else. You didn't leave them, did you?" Alicia inquired.

"Goodness no! I don't do that girly, rose stuff," Melanie said with a laugh.

"Well, someone did, and it's a little bit weird. Someone who either works here or knows someone who works here," Alicia said.

She looked around the store. Alicia could see that Danny was stealing looks at her. She wondered whether or not he was the culprit. After a bit of consideration, she decided to confront him on this.

"Hello, Danny," she said.

"Oh, hi there, Alicia. What's up?" he said, awkwardly scratching his head.

"Did you leave these flowers?" she asked.

"I saw them, and I thought you might like them," Danny said.

"I appreciate the thought, and I thank you. But I'd appreciate it if you didn't do that again," Alicia replied.

She walked away, seeing the annoyance on Danny's face. Alicia felt terrible, but then, he spoke.

"You know, that was my way of asking you to the light show this weekend if you wanna go," he said.

Seriously? Alicia turned to him, looking at him dead in the eye.

"I'm going with someone else. But I thank you for the offer," Alicia said.

The look in Danny's eyes said it all as Alicia went back to work. She never found him attractive, and the fact that he was acting like this made her feel slightly discomforted.

"Who? Some random guy?" Danny asked.

"It's none of your business, Danny. It's just someone I like and who makes me happy. I don't think I owe you any explanation," she said.

Alicia didn't want to explain it to Danny. She had a feeling he'd be jealous.

"So, you don't like me in that way?" Danny asked.

"I don't, Danny. I don't want to hurt your feelings or pride, but I'm not interested," she admitted.

It wasn't the first time he had asked her out. All through high school, he'd asked her. She would spend her time ignoring it, spending her time with Melanie instead. That alone should've been the hint.

"Fine. Have a good day then," Danny said.

He sulked off. For a moment, Alicia wondered if she was a little mean about turning him down. She didn't know for sure whether it was right to act like this toward him, mostly because she didn't want to be his girlfriend. However, he didn't take rejection like this very well. But, after she finished that conversation, he went back to work, and she felt a presence nearby.

"Hi, Melanie," she said.

"Hello back. Was Danny bothering you again?" Melanie asked.

"Yes. He asked me for a date, and I said no. He seemed upset. I wish he would understand and accept that I'm not into him," she said. Alicia had a bad habit of not being forceful with her words, but then, Melanie scoffed.

"You did nothing wrong. Danny should know by now that you're not his type. Your type is girls anyway," she said.

Alicia blushed.

"I never..." Alicia started to say but trailed off.

"I know it is, Alicia. Do you think I'm stupid? I can tell that you don't feel comfortable around most guys. But, around other women, you seem happier," she said to Alicia.

Alicia sat there, blushing crimson. She wondered if there was any way to make it work. But, for now, Alicia nodded.

"Yeah. I do. I just wish Danny would stop," Alicia said.

"Unfortunately, he's not the type to take a hint. So, unless you tell him you're gay, you're going to continue to be annoyed by him. Anyway, I have a meeting to go to in about an hour. Can you watch the store?"

"I certainly can," Alicia said.

Melanie left, and Alicia sighed. She was right. She knew that, especially if things with Melanie picked up, she would need to be honest with her feelings. For the rest of the day, Alicia watched the store, ignoring any comments from the others. When it was finally over, Melanie got ready for the date, heading back home and quickly changing to something warm. They both agreed to meet up at the skating rink, which was what Melanie preferred. She felt better just going there instead of meeting up at her place. It was quiet, and it still felt weird knowing that her mom wouldn't be home for a while.

That's because she was out trying to bang some guy.

The annoyance of her mother's antics did make Alicia tense, but she wanted to forget about it. After she composed herself, she went over to the skating rink. She saw Melanie sitting on one of the benches, a pair of skates in her hand, and a pair on her feet.

"There you are, I was about to call you," she said.

"You didn't have to get those for me," she said. She didn't expect Melanie to pay for the date.

"Relax, it's on me. Besides, you paid for coffee the last time. Did you forget that?" Melanie teased.

"Oh yeah," Alicia said.

"Anyway, let's get out there," Melanie said with a smile on her face.

Melanie stepped forward, and Alicia quickly tied the skates, hobbling over to the small cubby nearby and tossing them into there. She blushed as their hands touched one another, realizing that the little touches were making her heart flutter.

"Sorry," she said.

"Oh, it's fine. Quit being so nervous there, Alicia," Melanie said.

"Sorry, I just never thought that this would even happen. You know how it is," Melanie admitted.

"I know. But I care about you, Alicia. I mean, if I didn't, I wouldn't be here right now. So, there's that," she said with a smile.

Alicia looked over, flushing, and feeling nervous about everything. She had no idea how this would all go anyway, especially with the way things were.

"What about our friendship?" Alicia asked.

"I think our friendship will only get better if we stop being dishonest with ourselves," Melanie said with a smile.

Alicia then nodded, agreeing with her words. She took her hand and went out onto the ice. At first, it was nothing more than awkward grabbing. Then, Alicia learned how to stay upright without putting most of her body weight on Melanie. As she clung to

Melanie, she wondered if there was anything more she could do. Melanie held onto her. Alicia hugged Melanie's arm like a lifeline, holding onto her and refusing to let go.

Having Melanie here with her was a breath of fresh air, a bit different from what she was used to. She knew for a fact that Melanie cared a lot about her, and he'd both be happy together. Melanie felt pleased with the way she continued to steal glances at Alicia, but Alicia was also curious about where it would go.

What was the plan from here on out? Would they continue down the pathway of being just friends, but potentially being something more? Alicia wasn't against being more than just friends. She didn't want to jeopardize her friendship with Melanie. Any fears she had would go away when she skated with Melanie. Maybe Alicia was overthinking as per usual.

They skated for a long time, until about nine or so, and then, they turned in the skates. As Melanie took hers off, she looked at Alicia with a grin.

"The lights are just down the block. I had a wonderful time skating. You don't have to do much to have a good time with me," Melanie said.

"I did too. It's different, you know, hanging out like this," Alicia said.

"You mean as more than just friends? I'm going to be honest, Alicia. I was terrified to ask you out. I expected you'd say no," she said.

"What do you mean?" Alicia asked.

"I've always been nervous about asking you out. I never knew how you felt about me. I didn't want to ruin what was between us. I know I might come off as straight since I've only dated guys, but I've always liked you," she said.

"I feared pursuing anything with you because I knew that you have a lot of male admirers. And for a good reason. You are gorgeous," she said.

"You flatter me. But I think you're the cute one. You're always supportive, too, and I've always been happy about your accomplishments. Especially with your graphic design projects. You're still doing that, right?"

"Yeah. Trying to get a job in the field, but it's rough. I worry that I may suck, but I also think it's because I'm also a person in the field who isn't just trying to do crappy company work," she explained. Alicia did try to get over those boundaries, but they proved to be quite cumbersome.

"You should do what makes you happy. After all, I eventually want to do the same thing. You know, something that makes me happy," Melanie said.

"You're not happy working at the current place?"

Alicia asked.

"I like being in management. And, Ross, the owner has helped me a lot, but I don't know. I got offered a chance at the branch office, but I feel like pursuing that is just going to keep me away from my dream of having my own art studio, painting pictures that I enjoy. I want that," Melanie said.

Alicia completely understood Melanie and her reasons. That was why Alicia was working at the store. Her mom and feeling smothered.

"I truly understand. I feel that way with a lot of things," she said.

"Yeah. But when I'm with you, I feel like I can express myself. It's weird, I don't experience it with much else, but with you, it's like a whole new world, and it's something that I feel makes me happy, no matter what happens from here on out," Melanie said.

Alicia agreed with that.

"Yeah, no matter what happens, I'll always be your friend. I mean, I'm just happy you've stuck by me through thick and thin," she replied.

"Trust me. You need to do a lot to get rid of me."

Alicia smiled at those words. She felt happy, cared for, and, most of all, loved.

It was different. That was something Alicia rarely got outside of her personal projects, the compliments that she got from her friends on her work. Now, here she was with someone saying such wonderful things and supporting her. Alicia loved it.

Melanie walked over to the end of the block, and Alicia followed. They saw the array of pretty lights there, and Alicia felt a happiness she hadn't experienced in a long time. They walked toward the entrance and inside, seeing the glimmering lights there, a hand extended. It was Melanie's and Alicia took it. They walked through there, both of them staying mostly quiet, but Alicia felt a feeling of happiness that she never really experienced until now. It was nice, and it felt refreshing.

When they got to the big Christmas statue halfway into the park, Melanie turned to her, blushing crimson.

"By the way, Alicia, there's something I need to tell you. Something I've been holding out on until recently," she said.

"What do you mean?"

"What I mean is this."

Suddenly, Alicia was pulled in closer, causing her to let out a sudden gasp of surprise. What was Melanie doing? Suddenly, she was facing Melanie. The cold air around them, the other people ignoring them, all of it felt so surreal. But, in the flash of the lights, she suddenly felt a pair of soft lips against her own. Suddenly, Melanie was kissing her.

Melanie's kiss was so different from what Alicia expected. It was soft, sensual, and it felt perfect. She kissed her right then and there, expecting something to change. She thought that maybe some butterflies or something would come out and appear around them, but no, it was just the two of them together, both of them feeling the excitement of the moment. Melanie was heavenly to kiss, and for a long time, they just stood there, both of them kissing one another like there was no tomorrow.

Then, Melanie pulled away, looking at Alicia with a smile on her face. Alicia wondered what she would say or do next. What she did know for sure was that it was the best kiss ever, and she wanted nothing more than to experience it once again.

Chapter Six

For a moment, Melanie wondered how much her body was on autopilot. She never kissed a woman like that before, but it was magical.

Sweeter than a man's lips. When she pulled back, though, Melanie turned away in both shock and embarrassment.

"I'm so sorry!" Melanie said.

"For what? I didn't pull away," Alicia said.

"I know, but I didn't know if that was what you wanted. I'm not good at any of this. I felt like this was where you wanted the date to go, so I did what I had to do and—"

"You're fine, Melanie. You did the right thing, even if you think you didn't," Alicia said.

"Are you sure?" she asked.

"Yes. The truth is that I've wanted that for a while. I've had a crush on you since high school, but I was too scared to admit it," Alicia said.

"Really? Are you serious?"

Melanie asked.

"Yes. I really like you, Melanie. You're the first woman I've ever kissed. I've always liked you. I've wondered many times if maybe I'm just gay for you, but I'm not sure," Alicia said.

"Whatever the case, I'm just happy that you were honest with how you feel, Alicia. I feel the same way," Melanie admitted.

Melanie never thought things would come to that moment, with both of them confessing their feelings for each other. But then, Alicia smiled.

"You have nothing to worry about. I've thought about kissing you, among other things, for a long time. I'm not sure how to feel on it myself, but I honestly want to see where this goes," Alicia admitted.

"Are you sure? It's a new thing for both of us," Melanie said.

"Yeah. I'm sure. I mean, my place is open for the night. I'm not sure we want to bother your parents," Alicia said.

Melanie thought about it. Her family was pretty open, but she knew they'd be more interested in her getting another job rather than hearing about her new girlfriend.

"Okay, let's go to your place. I mean, I know what I'm doing with this, but if you have any insight...that's welcome too," she said.

"You're good. We'll take this slow," Alicia said.

Melanie didn't even know she felt like this until recently. She felt like her cheeks were flush red, and not just because it was cold out. It started to snow as they headed back, both of them staying close to one another. When they got to Alicia's place, she fumbled with the key, unlocking the door. When they entered, they both looked around.

"Wow, your mom still has everything set up as it did before," she said.

"Yeah. I'm not sure how my mom feels about you, but I don't think she'll be too mad about you staying over," she said.

"Right. Well, I am tonight, so my mom can't be too mad about it then," Alicia replied with a laugh.

"That's true," Melanie said.

They held hands as they gingerly walked up the stairs. Melanie noticed that Alicia's mom did put a Christmas tree up, but it was so barren and haphazardly done. It was apparent that Alicia's family was a bit of a mess. Melanie wanted to help, if only because her family was somewhat normal compared to this. But Melanie didn't want to overstep her bounds, especially with the way things were between them.

When they got over to where the bedroom was, Alicia awkwardly opened the door, feeling the redness on her face grow even more so as they slipped inside. Melanie noticed not much had changed. The anime posters were still up, the figurines were in the cabinet, and Melanie was surprised by it all.

"Wow, this is amazing," she said.

"Yeah. It's my little collection, but it makes me happy," Alicia said.

"We need to watch more anime together. I remember when we used to do that when we were younger. You know, before we got jobs and grew up," she said.

"I miss that as well," Alicia admitted.

They sat down on the bed; both of them awkwardly a few feet from one another. Melanie smiled and Alicia moved toward her.

"Well, here goes nothing," she said.

She moved in, kissing Melanie. Melanie responded, kissing her back with the same passion as before. The two of them stuck there together, just kissing, and Alicia seemed just as nervous as she was.

Melanie knew a little more about what to do in these situations because she did kiss guys. She started to press her tongue against Alicia's mouth, earning a shocked response from the brunette. But Alicia then let her tongue mingle with Alicia's, touching, teasing, and commingling with hers. The little moan that escaped Alicia's mouth was enough to drive her mad, and Alicia loved hearing this. It was always a treat to her, and always something that made her feel good.

The two of them continued for what seemed to be forever, kissing, touching, and teasing the other with their lips, tongue, and teeth. Alicia loved it. Melanie could tell from the little gasps and moans that escaped her mouth.

Alicia was then pushed onto the bed. Melanie began to kiss and explore Alicia's lips and mouth. Melanie moved her tongue slightly in and out of Alicia's mouth. They began to touch, tease, and caress each other. It felt amazing. Melanie decided to take things a little bit further.

Melanie didn't know how all of this went, but she was trying her best. She soon started to move her lips down Alicia's neck, lightly teasing her with soft, sensual touches. The little gasps of both shock and pure pleasure were enough to drive Melanie wild. She then started to gently nibble on Alicia, earning a moan of pleasure from Alicia as she did it. She bit down softly, but not enough to cause a Mark to appear, but enough to elicit a response from Alicia. She peppered kisses down her body, savoring the touch of it. She moved her hands to Alicia's coat, taking it off her body, leaving her in the green ugly Christmas sweater she had on, and the jeans she adorned.

Melanie didn't know what Alicia thought about what was going on. She moved back, looking at Alicia with a questioning glance.

"Are you okay with me continuing?" she asked.

"Yeah. I'm fine with it," Alicia said with a blush. Melanie could tell it was Alicia's first time, and she was still a nervous wreck. Alicia was interested in continuing, but nervous.

"Don't worry, I promise I'll take it nice and slow, and I won't hurt you," Melanie said.

"I believe you," Alicia replied.

Melanie could tell Alicia was nervous, feeling the slight tenseness in her body. But Alicia was enjoying it, moaning in response to Melanie's touches. Melanie then moved her hands to the bottom of Alicia's sweater, looking at Alicia for a moment.

It was the moment of truth. Melanie looked at Alicia as if to ask her if it were okay to continue. This moment would change their friendship. They wouldn't be just friends anymore.

And in a sense, Melanie liked that.

"Are you ready?" Melanie asked.

"Yes, I'm ready," Alicia said.

Melanie nodded, looking at Alicia before pulling her shirt up and tossing it over to the side. Alicia was wearing a pink bra, which held her sizable breasts. Melanie lightly moved her hands down, ghosting her fingers until they got to the very edge of Alicia's bra. She touched the edge causing Alicia to let out a sudden gasp of pleasure. Melanie smiled to herself, feeling excited about this.

Melanie knew that some women liked being touched in other ways besides the genitalia, and she figured out shortly after that Alicia was like that. Melanie dragged her lips down Alicia's body, letting them cascade all the way downwards until she got to the very edge of Alicia's bra. Melanie moved against Alicia's flesh, lightly kissing there and touching there. She watched with rapt delight as Alicia let out a sudden moan of pleasure, feeling her body tense and then relax with small, sensual sounds.

Melanie loved their lovemaking and knew Alicia was enjoying it as well. She then moved her lips down toward the edge of her breast, undoing the clasp on the bra and then tossing it off. Alicia looked at her with a blush on her face, her arms immediately heading toward the top half of her body, covering herself.

"You don't have to hide in front of me, Alicia," Melanie said with a purr.

"But—"

"I want to see you. I want to see you happy, Alicia," she said, her voice even and serious. Alicia looked at her with widened eyes, but then, she slowly extracted her fingers away, revealing her large, rounded orbs. She looked over at Melanie with a blush, and Melanie realized she was the most beautiful person she'd seen.

She kissed and touched Alicia's body, starting from her collarbone, and then moving toward her breasts, touching and teasing both large orbs and her nipples too. As she did this, Alicia let out a small moan of desire, lightly moving her hips upwards, and then relaxing once again. She then started to tease the outer circle of Alicia's nipples with her tongue, letting the tip lap against the nub shortly afterward. Alicia then cried out, lightly moving her hips upward as Melanie continued this. Melanie knew she was doing the right thing with this, and she knew that she was turning Alicia on, making her feel things that she hadn't felt before.

But then, Melanie grew curious. She wondered if she could make Alicia feel good down there. She moved her hands downwards, touching the very edge of Alicia's womanhood, touching there and lightly padding her fingers against the rim. Melanie watched as Alicia then started to whimper with delight. Alicia was at her mercy, and she loved everything about this. Alicia then began to spread herself. Melanie kissed down to the edge of her pants. She then moved to the button and fly of the jeans, undoing them and then lightly tossing them to the side as well.

When her eyes glazed over Alicia's body, she watched as she started to turn red, but Melanie noticed that Alicia was quite beautiful.

More beautiful than she thought possible. Alicia was a goddess, and Melanie felt like she was servicing the one god that she wanted to. Alicia was her type, and she loved seeing the little sounds that she made, and the reactions she possessed.

Alicia then started to cry out as Melanie moved her hands toward Alicia's legs, moving from the inner thighs over to the heat between her legs. She cupped it there, lightly touching the tips and watching with delight as Alicia then started to cry out, letting out a small yelp and moan of pleasure as she began to tease her lightly. Alicia was a mess at this point, moaning, crying out loud, and Melanie could tell this was the first time anyone had ever done anything like this.

That's why she opted to go slow.

She let her fingers drift downwards, touching the very edge of her womanhood. She then spread her apart, slipping a finger inside, and soon, she began pumping her fingers in and out of Alicia, watching with rapt delight as she started to cling to the sheets, screaming out with every single touch. Melanie started slowly but then began to move her fingers faster. It was enough to drive Melanie crazy, as well. She loved watching Alicia like this, and with every single touch, every single caress, and every single motion, she could see Alicia starting to come undone slowly.

Then Melanie moved her fingers upward, pumping faster, using her tongue as well to service Alicia. After a little bit, she noticed that Alicia was already growing tense once more. Alicia didn't have much stamina, which didn't surprise Melanie. She didn't have much strength left. It was then when, after a brief moment, Melanie pressed her hand toward Alicia's g-spot, causing Alicia to cry out, tense up and suddenly relax. It was like magic to watch.

Alicia had an orgasm. Melanie felt a strange sense of power, happiness, and well-being as she looked over Alicia, who seemed to be enjoying a treat.

"Did you enjoy that?" Melanie asked.

"It was wonderful Melanie. You sure you never did this before?"

"Nope. You're my first. I might've tried it on myself, but never like this. I enjoyed it," she admitted.

Melanie would be lying if she said it wasn't fun. She loved every moment of it, the fun of the satisfaction she saw on Alicia's face, the touch of her hands, and the way Alicia looked at her with complete, utter happiness with every single motion. Alicia was definitively happy, and Melanie felt the joy of this too.

Melanie then felt her body get pushed downwards, and soon, she was facing Alicia with a blush on her face.

"What are you doing?" she inquired. She didn't know what Alicia was doing.

"I'm returning the favor," Alicia said.

It was like magic. Alicia had her undressed from the waist down. Soon, Melanie's legs were open. Melanie thought that Alicia would do the same thing she did. Instead, Alicia waited a brief moment before pushing her face straight into Melanie's heat.

Melanie's eyes widened. Alicia was so good. She managed to touch and tease all the right spots. With each moment, Alicia was getting deeper and deeper within Melanie, touching her without any hesitation. Alicia was so good, and Melanie didn't know what to do about any of this. She stayed there, holding Alicia's head as she dug in, touching and teasing her.

Melanie gripped her head, holding it there as she thrust her hips up. She closed her eyes, squinting them as Alicia started to continue, licking and diving her tongue inside. When she finally hit that one spot, Melanie tensed up, gripping her head and crying out loud.

The sudden, thrilling feeling of her orgasm was something more significant than Melanie thought possible. For a moment, she felt like time had stopped. When she finally came back to reality, Alicia moved off of her. Of course, not before Melanie gave her a long, passionate kiss, both of them groaning in response to the feeling of each other. They stayed in that position until Alicia pulled away, flushing.

"That was wonderful," Alicia said.

"It was. I had a wonderful time. You did amazing, Alicia. For someone who has never made love, I was surprised how good you were at that," she said.

Alicia blushed. Melanie knew it was the first time Alicia had done anything like that.

"Nope. I never tried it. I wanted my first time to be with you," she said.

Alicia's words made Melanie blush. She smiled but couldn't believe it.

"Thanks, Alicia. I'm glad I waited too. I only knew what to do from movies. I mean, I only knew about kissing because a couple of guys I dated. It was different from what I thought, and I want to do it again," she admitted.

Alicia blushed. Melanie could tell even she didn't know what to do about anything, and she simply nodded.

"I do too. I loved it," Alicia said.

"I'd be happy to do it with you once more," Melanie said.

"I had a great time. We can keep this between us, at least for now. I think the last thing I want is my mom finding out everything," she said.

"Yeah. I know how it is for you. My parents are cool, but I know that they're still concerned about me not having a boyfriend. But for now, let's keep things as they are now. I had a good time," Melanie said.

"I did too. Anyway, I guess we can hang out here for a bit," Alicia said.

"Of course. I mean, your mom isn't coming back for a bit, right?"

"Yeah. Things might be weird in the morning if she is back, but who knows," she said.

"I don't think it'll be that bad. Anyway, let's get some sleep.

Melanie then patted the area of the bed next to her. Alicia climbed in. Melanie wrapped her arms around Alicia, holding it there and cuddling her. Alicia tensed up, but then, she suddenly relaxed. Melanie felt happy and ready for the future.

Alicia also had some lingering doubts. Things wouldn't be easy for either of them, mostly because Alicia's mom was a known homophobe. Perhaps, they could change the way she felt.

Alicia was happy, and Melanie wanted to keep it that way. Melanie would do anything to make Alicia happy and satisfied.

Chapter Seven

Alicia woke up the next morning to Melanie next to her. She lay there, remembering what she did the other night, smiling to herself.

There was a rustle of sheets next to her. Alicia looked over at Melanie, who was starting to wake up. The sounds of stretching came from the side of the bed.

"Are you awake?" Alicia asked.

"Yeah, barely. Did you sleep well?"

"Yes, I did. I wonder if my mom is back," she said.

Alicia went downstairs, noticing that her mom's coat and shoes weren't around. Alicia guessed that her mother spent the night with whatever guy she's seeing these days.

"She's not here?" Melanie asked.

"Nope. Not surprised, but at the same time, it is a little annoying," she admitted. Her mom was always like this, and it made her frustrated to know that this was happening.

"All right. I'll come downstairs there soon," Melanie said.

Alicia went downstairs to fix coffee. They were both off today, but as they sat there, Alicia wondered if her mother would figure it out, that they were together.

"So, what do you suppose we do now?" Melanie asked.

"I think it's best if we keep this quiet. You know how insane my mom is," she said.

"Yeah, that's the one downside. I like you a lot Alicia, but your mother is definitely a handful," she said.

"She'll probably come in here annoyed at me for something I didn't even do. As usual," Alicia said.

"I know how that feels. I'm trying to talk to my parents to see if we can figure out what to do next. I know they want me to stay with the company and take the branch office job, but I don't know. It's not my style. I would love to paint, but I don't get much of a chance to do it at home," she said.

"I mean, least they aren't hateful for your existence like mine," Alicia said.

"I know what we should do! We should try to leave this place. I know that it's hard, but I would love to get away. I wouldn't mind living on my own. I mean, I'm twenty-one. I should be able to now," Melanie said.

Alicia nodded. "I thought of that, but it's hard. I'm a broke college kid. I have two more years of school before I can safely leave with a degree. Plus, I don't have a job in a field I love. It's a bit heartbreaking. I'd love to leave, but I doubt that'll happen," she admitted.

"You're too down on yourself, Alicia. How about this. We try to get new jobs as soon as we can. I know that the holiday seasons are coming, but maybe we can find a way to escape. Even if it's after the first of the year, I would love that," Melanie said.

"Yeah. I'd love that too," Alicia replied. She was hesitant because she knew this idea would be a big deal with her mother.

"I'll try to work on it with my family, but I also want you to work on this too. Your mom has too much control over your life. You're an adult. If you pay rent here, you shouldn't be treated so poorly," Melanie said.

"Maybe you're right. I'm sick of trying to keep the peace when, in reality, I want to get out of here," Alicia said.

"Then leave Alicia. Do what makes you happy," she said.

Alicia knew she needed to do something. It was tearing her apart.

"Okay, let's plan on moving," she said.

"Perfect! Anyway, I need to get home. My family has been calling nonstop all day. I better find out what's going on," she said.

"Good luck. Your parents are probably worried about nothing," Alicia said.

"Right, I hope it's it," Melanie replied.

After they finished breakfast, Alicia walked Melanie to the intersection, where they usually part ways. Alicia looked at Melanie, blushing.

"Last night was wonderful. I want to do it again," Alicia said.

"I'd love that too. Let's settle for trying to get together over the next few days. If your mom found a new boyfriend, she'll probably be gone for a little while, right?"

"I doubt it, but worth a shot," Alicia said with a laugh.

They stood there, both of them realizing the closeness of their bodies. Alicia moved in, kissing

Melanie. Alicia and Melanie stood there, making out before Alicia pulled away, flushing.

"Anyway, I've got to go," Alicia said.

Alicia then headed back home. When she got back, her mom was there, on the couch, and looking satisfied.

"There you are. Where did you go?"

Alicia's mother asked.

"I was saying goodbye to a friend. I told you Melanie came over," she said.

"Oh, her," Alicia's mom said.

"Why are you so against her, Mom? I thought you liked me having friends."

"I don't know. I worry she's a bad influence on you. Having a woman around like that is going to scare away all the guys. She's so bossy too," she said.

"I don't think she's bossy at all," Alicia said. She thought her mom was a little hypocritical with that statement, but that was beside the point.

"Anyway, I have another date with a guy. Have you had any luck in finding another job?"

"No, but I'm trying," Alicia said.

"Well, you need to pull your weight around here. I can't keep doing this," her mother said.

Alicia looked at her mom.

"You do realize I pay for most of the bills around here? You don't give a damn that I do all this work. You just want to go out and go on joyrides with your boyfriends, right?" she said.

Alicia's mother looked at her, standing up and glaring.

"Excuse me! Whose name is the apartment in? My name. You better back off, or I'm going to make you pay for what you said," Alicia's mother snapped.

"You don't do anything around here. I'm sick of always having this discussion with you. I've decided to find a new job and leave. You don't care about anyone but yourself. To think, it's the Christmas season, and you're still a selfish bitch," Alicia said.

"Watch your tone, young lady!"

"I'm not a child. Fuck off!"

Alicia was so tired of her mom. She was always nagging on her, making her feel like garbage. As Alicia got to her room, tears flooded down her face. She went to the computer, checked her emails to see if anyone had sent any follow-up emails.

Rejection, rejection, rejection. All of this was the same tune, different words. Alicia thought about giving up since she was going to be in school for two more years. She did it online, but it was still so hard to even find anything.

As Alicia surfed the web, she started to find a job that might be good for her. She read over it, eyes widening in realization.

"No way," she said to herself.

She read it over again a couple of times, realizing that this ad was definitely what she thought it was. It was a job to work as an intern for one of the top animation companies in the area. She read over the fine print, realizing she'd be making double what she'd be making at the store, and it was a good job that worked with her schedule.

"This has to be my new job. It just has to," Alicia said to herself.

Alicia never went after these sorts of jobs. She always thought she was too inexperienced to get a substantial job such as that. But Alicia closed her eyes, took a leap of faith as she filled out the application, supplying all of the relevant information.

Alicia put down that she was a student and that she was looking for a job to help her portfolio while she was pursuing her degree. It would be an excellent way to build experience. She wondered what might happen if she did that, and what might occur.

Alicia then sent it after reading it over a few times and changing a few things here and there. When she pressed send, she then closed her eyes, breathing out.

If she got this job, she would cry. Alicia could finally leave and work for others. She could finally live her own life. She wondered if Melanie would like to join her. Moving out would be a little hard at first, but Alicia also looked into campus apartments. While most of her classes were online, she did have one class on campus next month.

Alicia searched the rental ads and found one potential apartment. She realized that it would be right within her budget. It was almost as much as she was paying her mom for everything. Taking another leap of faith, she applied for the apartment. If worst came to worst, she could take a holiday job.

Alicia felt happy. She felt like life was changing for the better, and that deep down, everything would be okay. Alicia wanted to feel secure with her life choices. So, she hoped that with these changes, everything would be all right.

Chapter Eight

Melanie headed to her home, wondering what her parents wanted. Judging from the calls and texts, it was something big. When she got home, she saw her mom there.

"There you are, we've been waiting for you," she said.

"What's the matter, Mom?"

"It's your father. He fell and hurt his head. Your grandma is with him currently, but we need to go to the hospital," she said.

"How did it happen?"

"Putting up Christmas lights. I'm sorry for calling you so suddenly when you were with your friend, but I think this is important," she said.

"What happened to him?"

"We don't know. All I know is I heard a thud, and I went outside, found your dad there, and rushed him to the hospital. It's the hospital right down the street. I asked for them to keep me updated while I waited for you," her mother said.

Melanie nodded.

"I hope he's okay," Melanie said.

"He will be. Your dad is strong. I believe it'll be all right," she said.

Melanie nodded. "Right. I'll come over there.

Melanie raced to the hospital with her mom. When she entered your father's room, he was barely conscious. Melanie grasped his hand, holding it there.

"Hey, Dad. It's me. Sorry for being so late," Melanie said.

"You're fine. It's okay," Melanie's dad said.

"I was trying to get here as fast as I could," she said.

"I'm glad you made it out here. Don't think this will be the end of your old dad," he said.

"I know, but you worry me," she said.

"Don't worry about me. It's going to take a lot more to bring me down," he said.

Melanie's mom nodded.

"He'll recover. Christmas is going to be a little rough this year,"

Melanie's mother asked.

"Why is that?" Melanie asked.

"Well, he's going to be out of work. That means less money for presents," she said.

Melanie listened to her mom.

"Right. I'll help however I can. I mean, it's only fair," she said.

"Good. You're a good kid, Melanie. By the way, how did it go with Alicia last night?" she asked.

Melanie looked at her mom and dad. They were supportive in everything besides her artistic endeavors. However, they didn't know that she was gay. They were always teasing her about a boyfriend, but Melanie knew that deep down if she didn't tell her parents about Alicia, she'd regret it.

"Can I tell you both something important?" Melanie asked.

"Of course. You can always come to us," her mom said.

Melanie felt the nervousness course through her body as she listened to them, feeling the fear of the moment. At the same time, she knew that if she didn't do something about it now, it might be too late.

"I'm actually with Alicia. She's my girlfriend," she said.

Melanie's mom and dad both looked at one another. For a moment, then they nodded.

"I see. We figured out that you liked Alicia a little bit," her mom said.

"Do what makes you happy. You may not be around long enough to tell the tale," her father said.

Melanie's eyes widened. They seemed so calm about it.

"You're not mad?" she asked.

"Why would we be mad? A person can't help who they fall in love with. Isn't she the woman who is kind of strange but likes anime? She's a good kid," her mom said.

Alicia was a strange woman, but she was also a good friend. Melanie heard those words, shock settling in.

"She's a weird woman who likes anime, but are you both okay with it? Really?" Melanie asked.

"Of course. It's your life, your choices," her father said.

"Indeed. There's no harm in being with someone who makes you happy. We banked on you not having grandkids anyway," her mom said.

Melanie listened to them, shocked they were so calm and unaffected by it all.

"Would it be okay for me to bring her to Christmas?"

"Sure. Just understand that while we do support your choices in that regard, we still want you to get a good job. We want you to have something that makes you happy. We'll let you paint and do what you love, provided you work toward a better future with the company you're at," her mom said.

Melanie listened to them, surprised they were okay with this. They were so supportive and it made her feel good.

"Thank you. I really do appreciate it. I'll let you know what Alicia says, if that's okay."

"Wonderful," her mother said.

"I'm tired. The antibiotics are kicking in," Melanie's father said.

"I should get going. I have to tell Alicia what happened," she said.

"Now remember what we said. Focus on your career and build that," her mother said.

Melanie smiled. She would do that. Even though she didn't want to take the offer, Melanie thought working for the branch office would be okay.

***

After she left the hospital, Melanie contacted the branch office.

"Pewter's Industries. This is Mary. How may I help you?"

"Hello, this is Melanie Morris. I called to let you know that I've given it some thought and decided to take your offer," she said.

There was a pause, and Mary spoke.

"Perfect. A quicker answer than I thought. You can come in and start training after the first of the year," Mary said.

"Thank you," she said.

"You're very welcome. We're excited to have you on the team," Mary said.

Long gone would be the days of working with less than happy customers. Melanie felt terrible for leaving Alicia, but maybe she was making the appropriate changes too.

She called Alicia. The first couple of times, it went straight to voicemail. On the third try, Alicia picked up.

"Hi," Alicia said.

"Hi. I have some news. I wanted to talk to you in person. When are you free?" Melanie asked.

"I have a couple of freelance animation projects to do today. Maybe Tuesday? I work tomorrow and Monday."

"I work every day, but Tuesday next week. Let's do it then. I think it's something that's better discussed not in front of others, if that's cool with you," she said.

"Perfect for me," Alicia said.

Melanie hung up and immediately went home to paint. She kept her materials hidden for so long. Now, Melanie was working at the easel for the first time in quite a while. She wondered if she could make some side cash with her paintings. She wasn't going to make this her primary job. Perhaps her family was right. For now, though, she was just happy to have this option, and to make the changes she wanted to.

Chapter Nine

Alicia felt happy. She was pleased she was making changes, but she was still stuck with her mom.

Her mother was at work once again, leaving her alone. Alicia wanted to do some exploring. There was something about her whole situation in life that had always irritated her. She wanted to know the truth.

Alicia was looking for information on her dad. It was something she wanted for a long time and something Alicia desired to discover. When she tried searching the internet, nothing would show up. Then she got the idea.

Her mom had to have something in her divorce papers. Alicia waited until her mom was gone before heading into her room.

Alicia knew if her mother found out, she would kill her. Alicia wondered if maybe she was onto something. Alicia looked in the closet, taking the bras and boots that were haphazardly tossed in there and keeping them in the corner. So far, there wasn't anything, but then, after a second, she found another item.

"Jackpot," she said. It was a box, and it said: "Documents, Don't Touch!" Of course, Alicia was going to touch them. She was going to rummage through them.

Alicia checked to see if the coast was clear before looking through the box. At first, she found just unhelpful items, like birth certificates, quietly taking her own and her health records. Then, she noticed something sticking out.

"Divorce proceedings," Alicia said.

This was the divorce information between her father and mother. She quickly opened it, looking through the contents. Sure enough, this was what she wanted. It contained her father's contact info, address as of last year, and other information. Her mother held onto this. It made her realize that she was hiding something, and it had to be significant.

"What is she keeping from me?" she asked herself.

Alicia took the information, also looking into why they divorced. It said because of personal differences. But, in the corner, it said sexuality. Alicia wondered about it, but she decided to ignore the information.

However, the one thing that shocked her was the address. Her father lived right down the road. Her mother had kept that from her the entire time! As Alicia grabbed the information, she thought about what to do with it.

Alicia could either leave, find out if her dad was there, learn the truth, and go from there. Or, she could ignore it since it might get her in more trouble, especially if her mom found out that she knew the truth.

Alicia grabbed her jacket. She wasn't going to ignore the information and pretend that her mom could be so secretive.

With nothing to lose, Alicia made her way to the address, which was a mere thirty-minute walk. The fact that her dad was so close and she never knew it, bothered her deeply.

When Alicia got to the entrance, she stopped, looking at the doorway. She pressed the doorbell. Suddenly, there was the sound of someone inside. She heard "Who could that be" in the distance, but

Alicia couldn't tell if the tone was a good thing or not. The sound of someone coming to the door echoed until finally, the door opened. A bespectacled man looked at Alicia with widened eyes.

"Alicia?"

"Dad?"

"Oh my gosh! It's been so long!" Alicia's dad said.

"Yes, it has," she said.

"Come on in. I was wondering when you'd figure it out. We can talk about it in here," he said.

Alicia ambled inside, and she noticed a cute apartment decorated in a country style. There was another man about her father's age there, with blond hair, black glasses, and wearing a blue, long-sleeve shirt.

"Bruce. This is my daughter Alicia," he said.

"Bruce? Is he your—"

"Husband. I got remarried after your mother and I divorced. About five years ago," he said.

Alicia looked at her dad, and then back at Bruce. He looked so similar to her dad. It was a bit odd, but she simply nodded.

"Wow. I didn't know you were—"

"Gay? Yes, I am. That's one of the reasons why your mother and I divorced. She became very hateful toward me," he said.

"I can imagine. She's a controlling bitch," Alicia said.

"I'm not going to deny that. Is your mother home right now? I wanted to see you, but you know how she is with agreements. I was about to take legal action. It was messy, but she won. I had to pay child support. I hoped that once you became a legal adult, we could discuss this as a family. I could let you decide how you wanted to approach our relationship, but I know she wouldn't do that. I wanted to give you a choice, Alicia, but I don't think that happened," he said.

Alicia shook her head. "No, she's a controlling bitch, sleeping with every other guy each night, and then is mad when I tell her I applied to another job to be an animator," she explained.

"That's your mom, all right. I wish I knew where you guys were," he replied.

Alicia paused.

"So, she didn't tell you? We are right down the street. It was a thirty-minute walk," she said.

"Well, I'm both disappointed and not surprised. Your mom didn't take well to being honest about things. One of them was her relationship with me," he said.

Alicia sat down, feeling nervous. She never really got a chance to hear about this. Right now, her dad was sitting here, about to tell her everything.

"You can tell me, Dad. I'm willing to listen," she replied.

"Alicia, I'm kind of a shitty person myself. I didn't tell your mom how I felt. Our marriage was a disaster. I only stuck around because I wanted to raise you. But that didn't happen. I ended up realizing when I was with your mom; I was never happy. She always had something to get on my case for. I honestly got tired of it. I got freaking tired of it. I asked her if she really loved me. She said she did. Then, I found all the numbers of other guys she 'claimed' weren't a problem. I was pretty damn hurt. When I told her that we were through, she got very upset with me. But I was tired of being led on by her. I know that I never told you, but she said we should do it without upsetting you. You were a child at the time," he said.

"Wow. I didn't realize it hurt you so much. I'm sorry for not coming around sooner, Dad. I only found out the truth because Mom was gone," she said.

"Yeah. I know it's hard. I'm sorry for not being honest with you, Alicia. I wanted to figure out how to call you, but I didn't want to scare you away. I didn't know what your mom said about me, either. She probably thinks I'm the terrible one when it was her," he said.

"Oh, she does. She hates you, Dad. The thing is, I don't. I really don't hate you at all. In fact, I want you to be a bigger part of my life. I want to leave her place," she said.

Alicia truly meant every word she said to her father. She had thought about having a relationship with him for a long time. Her dad's brows furrowed.

"Does she know? That you want to leave?" Alicia's dad asked.

"Yeah, she does. I got a little agitated and told her I didn't want to stay there. She threatened me with calling the police and having me kicked out," she explained.

"Typical Nicki. I swear, I'll take you in myself if I have to," he said.

Immediately, Alicia looked at him.

"Would you like to stay with me? Just until you get yourself sorted out? I can help in whatever way you need. I don't know if you're really into the helicopter parent, but I can provide my own set of help as needed," he said.

"I wouldn't mind that," she replied. Alicia was jumping for joy inside. Her dad looked at her, a fleeting grin on his face.

"Don't lie to me, Alicia," he said.

Alicia immediately tensed. "What are you talking about?"

"You aren't just going to like it. I can see it in your eyes. You're happier than ever before," Alicia's father said.

"I am, Dad. I am much happier," she replied.

"Well, if you want to get away from her, and you can do it secretly, I'll help you. You're going to have to do it during a day she's working that you're not, though. And keep our conversation between us if you can," he said.

Alicia nodded. "I wouldn't dare tell her. She doesn't need to know. I wish I sought you out sooner. I wanted to get away, and I just thought you didn't want to be near me or deal with me. I thought I was just your kid, and that was it," she said.

Alicia remembered her dad getting along decently with her when she was younger. She thought that time might have ended up causing a rift. But her dad shook his head, looking directly into her eyes. He took a deep breath, and then he spoke.

"I'm going to be honest with you, Alicia. I thought about just going there and taking you away myself. Your mom is so hateful, especially against gay people. I think it's partially due to our relationship, but she was hateful beforehand. She makes fun of people and criticizes them. I hated it. I didn't want to see you suffer, nor did I want to be in the position where I had to deal with that," he said.

"So, what you're saying is..."

"Your mom is going to hate you if you come out. I suggest doing it after you leave. You will always have a place here if you're worried about that," he replied.

Alicia nodded. "Thanks, Dad. It'll be sooner rather than later. But I want to hear back on this job before I make the change," she replied.

"Fine by me. Just stay in touch. You know where I live. I'll help how I can," he said.

Alicia grinned. She spent the rest of her day with her dad, realizing that everything her mom said about him was, of course, entirely and utterly wrong. He was a good guy. He cared about his family, even though he couldn't show it to anyone for a long time. She realized that her dad was trying his best to be a good father. But there were definitely some issues with the way things went. Alicia was just happy. She was ready and determined to have a brighter future, even if she had a few obstacles in the way.

Chapter Ten

Melanie spent the next couple days with her dad in the hospital, happy that he was doing better. She went to the store on Monday, noticing that Braydon and Danny were already hard at work.

"Is Alicia here yet?" she asked.

"Nope. Haven't seen her," Brayden said.

"Weird, she's not the type to be late. I hope everything is all right," she said.

Melanie waited for about an hour. Suddenly, Alicia showed up. Her head was down, but Melanie quickly realized something happened.

"Alicia? Are you okay?" she asked.

"Not really. I don't want to talk about it," Alicia said.

"Are you sure?"

"I don't. It's hard to explain. I know if I tell anyone about it, I'll just get in trouble," Alicia said.

The atmosphere of the store changed. Danny looked at Alicia, running toward her with concern.

"Alicia, is everything all right?" Danny asked.

"I told you not to worry," she snapped.

Alicia clocked in and started doing her job.

Melanie was not used to this. She was so sure that Alicia was doing better. When they parted ways, everything seemed as fine as they could be. But now, Alicia was randomly lashing out at people, and Melanie wasn't in the mood to deal with it.

Alicia was quiet, ignoring almost everyone but customers. Melanie noticed that Alicia was spending her time alone.

"Alicia I—"

"Please don't talk to me right now. I have a lot on my mind," she said.

"Alicia, you don't have to do this. We can talk this out like adults," Melanie said.

"I really don't want to. I'm busy," Alicia replied.

"That's bull, Alicia. You were fine. Something has changed," she said.

Alicia looked at her.

"My mom is not treating me well," she said.

"Is she abusing you?"

Alicia looked around, waiting a moment before pulling her stomach up. There, a red welt decorated her skin.

"You can thank my mom for this. She punched me in the gut when we were fighting. She's terrible. I don't know what to do about it. Things have changed for me, but I'm scared," she said.

"Alicia, you have nothing to worry about," she replied.

"Yes, I do Melanie! I don't know how much more I can take. I'm being driven crazy. And I...I met my dad the other day," she explained.

Alicia's dad? But Melanie always thought he was just a drunkard, and that was the reason why Alicia lived with her mom.

"Isn't your dad abusive?"

"Not at all! He's just gay. He has a loving husband, and they're so happy. I feel different and powerless at the moment," Alicia said.

"Maybe we can work this out together. Do you need help," she asked Alicia. Melanie didn't know how much she could do. Alicia couldn't live with her, but if she needed assistance in standing up to her mom, she would be there in a heartbeat.

"I just need a callback on this job. I applied to an animation position. I want it so badly, Melanie. I'm trying so hard. I want to leave," she said.

Melanie extended her arm, wrapping it all around Alicia and from there, squeezing her tightly. Alicia moved inside, enjoying the feeling of her arms, and Melanie simply held her there.

"Alicia, no matter what happens next, please know that I'm here for you. No matter what," she said.

"I know you are Melanie. You've been there for me for a long time," she said.

"I know. Actually, I told my family about you. They are happy, and they accept our relationship. They just told me that if you want to come over for Christmas, you're welcome to," Melanie offered.

Alicia's eyes widened.

"Are you sure?"

"Yes. I also took the job at the branch office. I'm not going to leave you behind or anything but let's face it, Alicia, it's too good to be true," she said.

"But we won't be working together," she pointed out.

"Maybe I can work out something with the branch office. But this is better. I'm happy, and if you're going into animation, I would like for you to get that job. Don't stay here. We can replace ourselves, but we can't replace the feelings that we have, and our dreams and aspirations," Melanie said.

It wasn't an ideal job. It wasn't even the best job, and Melanie felt like it was just another rung on the corporate ladder. She was ready to take this step forward. She looked over at Alicia, who had tears in her eyes.

"You promise this won't change things between us?" Alicia asked.

"Of course not. I don't want to lose you, Alicia. I want to spend my life with you if I can. I don't want to hold ourselves back because of the troubles of our past. I want to embrace the future, even if the future is a little bit chaotic," Melanie pointed out.

Alicia looked at her, pausing for a second. Melanie could tell that Alicia was trying to figure out what to do next. It was different for her, mainly since Alicia was used to always having her around.

"I'm going to miss you, but I accept it. My dad offered me a chance to live with him and his husband. I don't want to burden him. I'd love it if I got the job, and from there, I could figure out what to do next. That would make everything all the easier," Alicia explained.

"Well, I have faith that they will. I'm going to try to get my business off the ground too. I would love just to leave the world of retail and work on my art, but I'm not going to do that without an exit plan," she explained.

Melanie knew better than this. She knew the field of the arts was only getting bigger and bigger, and she didn't want to be just another bump on a log. She wanted to make a difference with her art and to make it work.

"Okay. Let's hope for the best for one another. It'll be the Christmas gift we've been waiting for," Alicia said.

"For sure. Let's fix our lives so we can finally have the one we want, and not be held back by the overbearing standards of society," Melanie said.

The two of them sat there, giving one another kisses. Then, there was the sight of someone in the distance. Melanie looked up, lightly moving away.

"Someone is watching us," Melanie said.

She got up with Alicia following after her. She walked toward the bushes. Suddenly, someone ran out, barreling through the shopping center. Melanie broke out into a run, chasing after the guy.

She felt her pulse beat faster, the thrill of the energy in her body pushing her forward. Melanie's legs stung in pain and exhaustion, but she wasn't going to give up. She would stay in this race and get the bastard who was creepily taking pictures.

The person went over to one of the hallways. Melanie knew that it would be a dead-end there. She was glad that her cross-country practices from high school still paid off. Suddenly, the unknown person stopped. When she got there, her eyes widened.

"Danny?" Melanie said.

"Yeah. It's me. I caught you. I knew that Alicia was off in la-la land with someone, but I didn't expect you," Danny said.

"What the hell are you doing? You should know by now stalking is creepy and very wrong," Melanie spat.

"Well, I'm here to make a deal with you," he said.

"What kind of deal?"

"It's simple. You give me the job, and I won't bring this photo around the office. I'm sure people will love seeing their new branch manager with her girlfriend," Danny said.

That bastard! He wouldn't. As Melanie was close to kicking his ass, a voice rang out.

"Melanie, don't let it bother you. I'll take care of this," Alicia said.

"What are you—"

"Leave us alone, Danny. I know why you're doing this," she said.

"I'm doing it because I've tried so hard to get your attention, and you don't even care. You care so much more about this bitch than you do me. I've been your friend for a long time, Alicia," he said.

Melanie looked at Alicia, realizing that the ball was in her court. No matter what Melanie said this guy was doing, it wouldn't mean anything because Alicia was trying to make a point to this guy.

"Listen here, Danny. I understand why you're upset. But this isn't the way to go about saying what you want to say. I understand why you feel this way, why you think the world is so cold, why it sucks, but this isn't what you should be doing. You need to honest with yourself, Danny. Neither of us wants a relationship. I don't like you in that way, Danny. I never have, and I hate that you don't seem to get it, but so be it," she said.

"I was going to ask you out during the Christmas lights. But I see that this dyke ass bitch has one-upped me," Danny said.

Melanie looked at Alicia.

"Give him the final words. Tell him that you're not interested. I've got to make some calls," Melanie said.

Melanie had the recording of Danny's words. While it was a little bit underhanded to do this, she wasn't going to sit there and have Danny insult her girlfriend. Melanie called Human Resources and explained the situation. They asked for the voice file, which is what Melanie gave to them.

When she came back, she saw Alicia in the corner, with Danny right over her, threatening her with something.

"Hey!" Melanie said.

Danny turned toward her. Melanie curled her lips into a smile.

"While you were busy threatening my girlfriend, I called HR. They found out about our little venture. They won't tolerate hate speech and threats. So, Human Resources is expecting you in the corporate office tomorrow at 9 a.m. sharp, ," Melanie said.

Danny looked at both of them like they had four faces.

"You didn't—"

"Oh, but I did. I contacted HR, told them how I felt and told them that you were threatening the livelihood of multiple employees. So, have fun with Human Resources, asshole," Melanie said.

Melanie knew it was dicey on whether or not that was an abuse of power. But, at the same time, she really didn't care. Melanie was just happy about making a change like this. She looked at Danny, who was grimacing, and for a bit, they simply stood there, looking at one another.

"You can leave Danny. We're together, deal with it," Melanie said.

"Yeah, Danny, I haven't liked you for a while. You've kind of creeped me out," Alicia said.

He looked at them, and Melanie wondered if he was going to try anything more, but then he stopped.

"Right. I'll be going now," Danny said to them.

He then walked away, and Melanie smiled at him.

"Did we just do that?" Alicia said.

"Yes, someone needed to stand up to him. I was getting pretty damn tired of him always bothering you and making it uncomfortable for you," Melanie said.

"Right. I felt the same way," she said.

"Listen, Alicia. I'm not the best at this, but I just want to say I'm happy to have you, and I want you to do well. I chased off Danny. So, let's get our lives together before the new year starts," Melanie said.

"I'll do my best, Melanie. You've inspired me to go forward and not let my mom hold me back."

"And that's how it should be, Alicia. You shouldn't be held back," she replied.

Alicia nodded, and for Melanie, she felt happy, ready to start on the future, and satisfied. She went home after her shift, getting her easel out. She started to paint because she had a feeling what she wanted to paint was relevant to her relationship with Alicia.

The future was looking brighter than ever. Things were falling into place now, Alicia just needed to confront her demons, and win. Once she did that, the rest of this would be smooth sailing. They'd figure it out in their own way. Alicia was here for her, and she was there for Alicia. Melanie would do everything in her power to keep their relationship happy for both of them.

Hiding wasn't an option anymore. Melanie would build a better, more worthwhile life for both of them.

Chapter Eleven

Alicia felt inspired after hearing Melanie eagerly telling her to live her own life. It gave her a lot of happiness, both inside and outside. As she went to her apartment, she got a call. She picked it up, holding it to her ear.

"Yes. Who is it?"

"Is this Alicia Ward?" the voice asked.

"Yes. Who is this?" she said.

"My name is Marcos Colt. I'm the head of animations here at Bingsley Animated. We received your resume, and I have to say, I'm very impressed! You're local too! We wanted to contact you about the application you submitted. For the internship," he said to her.

Alicia stopped and almost dropped her books at that point. There was no way this was happening.

"You don't mean—"

"Yes, Alicia. We'd like for you to join our team," he said.

She stood there for a moment, realizing just what was going on. She started to feel her heart race, her body shocked by everything that was transpiring. She couldn't believe it.

No, she could.

She definitely could. Maybe this was fate finally giving her something to feel happy about.

"You mean this, right? It's not just a dream?"

"Course not, Miss Ward. We want you on the team. We reviewed your work. You're astounding," he said.

The way he said those words made Alicia's heart flutter slightly. She really did feel happy. She was definitely inspired.

"Thank you. Thank you so much," she said to him.

"You're welcome. So, we won't be able to start you off until the beginning of the year, if that's okay with you. That does, however, give you enough time to turn in your two weeks at any previous jobs, and spend time with your family during the holidays, if that's what you desire," he said.

"Yes, I'd love for that to happen," she said.

"Well then there you go. You'll be with us starting the first of January. You can come in and sign the offer at any time," he said.

"Thank you. I certainly will," Alicia said.

She ended the call, realizing what was going on. She could leave her home now if she wanted to. She wanted to discuss this with Melanie first, because she worried what might happen when she did leave. She knew if she came forward to her mom about it now, things would erupt.

Alicia wasn't tied to any lease with her mom. Her mom was the only one on it, which meant she could legally kick Alicia out, since she was an adult. She wouldn't put it past the woman, that's for sure.

After Alicia practically jumped for joy, she called Melanie.

"Hey Mel. So uh, things have changed," she said.

"What do you mean?"

"I got the job," Alicia said.

"You mean..."

"The one for the animation company! I couldn't believe it myself, but they said they wanted me to start in January," she said to Melanie.

"Wow! That's so awesome! Congrats!" she said to Alicia.

Alicia smiled to herself. She felt like she was finally making a name for herself, even with all of the chaos that was going on. She felt good, she felt happy, and most of all, she felt inspired to do so much more. Alicia didn't feel like she was stuck in a dead-end job anymore.

But it also meant she'd have to talk to her dad about this. Alicia called her father and waited a brief moment. Suddenly, she heard the sound of his voice.

"Alicia? What's the matter? Are you okay?" he asked.

"Of course, Dad. I just wanted to tell you some good news. I got the job with that animation company I wanted to work for," she said.

"Are you serious?"

"Yes. They called me and told me I got the job. I start at the first of the year," she said.

"Wow. That's amazing!"

She smiled to herself. Alicia felt happy knowing that her dad actually supported her endeavors. She'd gone far too long not to get a chance to do this, and she felt happy, and satisfied too.

"Anyway Dad, I feel really happy. I just wanted to tell you. I know how we talked about me moving in, but I really didn't want to until there was full confirmation that I'd get the job," she said to him.

"No, that's amazing! I love it," he said to her.

"Yeah, I'm glad. So, is it still okay if I live with you till I have enough for my own place, and then if things are good with Melanie and me, I move in with her?" Alicia asked.

She hoped her dad still meant it. She was worried that there might be a change, but then, she heard a chuckle.

"You really think I would toss you to the corner like that Alicia? Of course, you're welcome to stay with me for as long as you need it. I don't want you to be tossed away by your family or anything. I'm still here, even if your mom would rather forget my existence," he said.

"Right. Thank you, Dad for everything. I'm not sure when I want to move yet, but I want it to be before Christmas. I don't want to spend it with her. She'll probably be with some guy anyway, and I'll be left alone," Alicia said.

"Well, if you can't do it before then, you're welcome to spend Christmas with us, and Melanie is welcome too," he said.

Alicia nodded. There was so much going on, so many changes, and so much to do. She definitely felt like she was going to feel better with this decision, since it allowed her to get the results she wanted.

"Thank you so much Dad. I really do mean it. I know things weren't easy for us, but I appreciate your help with everything. It's a big change, but it's a good one," she admitted.

"I know Alicia. I'm proud of you. No matter what happens next, we've got this," he said.

"We do, Dad. That I'm sure of," she replied.

The feeling of happiness, of love from a parent, made Alicia want to cry. Her dad was so supportive, and she felt like there was something else that was happening to her. Alicia felt happy, she felt satisfied, she definitely was ready for action. She wanted nothing more than to just move forward with her life.

There was still one more thing to do, and that was to say goodbye to her mom for good. She wanted to break it to her with Melanie, that she was tired of the abuse, and the hurt, but she didn't want to do it yet. She would bide her time until things settled.

Chapter Twelve

For Melanie, the idea of her new job, her new life, and her future, made her utterly happy. Her dad was out of the hospital, and Melanie spent most of her time when she wasn't at the studio with him.

The fall made things hard on him. He struggled with doing most things, and despite his tenacity, she could see him suffering.

"Don't worry about me Mel. You're fine," she said.

"But Dad, you can barely walk," she snapped.

"I'm fine, stop worrying about me, dear," he said.

Melanie always dealt with this. Her dad was a great guy, but it certainly wasn't easy for her to deal with him still acting like that. She felt like he was a bit too headstrong. He went over to the kitchen to fix himself food, even though the doctors said to keep off his feet for a bit.

"Come on Melanie, I'm getting older. I don't need you to worry about me so much," he said.

"Dad, you know that I'm supposed to be taking care of you when Mom isn't here. I managed to get a few days off by a stroke of luck and—"

That's when Melanie saw it and a look of horror appeared on her face.

"No Dad, please don't go there," she said, crying as she saw her dad move toward the studio. She hadn't shown anyone the art she'd been doing. She made a little bit of income with this, and when her dad opened the door, he looked at the sight.

"Wait a second, this isn't the bathroom," he said.

"No Dad. That's my studio," she said to him.

She watched as he looked inside, a bit of surprise on his face.

"You do art?"

"Yes. I've kept it a secret from everyone because I don't want anyone to know and judge me," Melanie admitted.

Melanie also didn't want her family to think she was lazy or anything. But then, he looked around, gasping at the sights.

"This is just, wow," he said to her.

"You think so?"

"Yes! This is wonderful Melanie. Have you shown your mother?"

"Of course not. She told me not to focus on art. And so did you," she said.

"Well, I didn't want you only to do art. I want you to continue school, Melanie. But, if you want to, you're more than welcome to sell these, and do it as a side gig," he said.

Melanie blushed.

"That's kind of what I've been doing, at least to help make a little more money since you were off work. I did take the new job. I don't intend to leave this house either until I'm fully stabilized, but I also feel like I could make some money with these. I don't want it to be a job either," Melanie said.

"You don't? But I thought you liked it!"

That's when Melanie said the truth. She did realize she loved art, to the point where she didn't want to lose the spark and the drive of this. She wanted to spend more time doing art, and she definitely was a bit surprised by the way that this felt.

"I do Dad, but...I guess you two were warning me that day about pursuing it. Sometimes, part of the reason why you warn your kids is so they don't get upset when they do pursue it as an art. It's a bit weird, but I get it now," she said.

"You're right. I think you get it. I've been concerned about you pursuing it. You can if you want to. At the end of the day, you're the one choosing your fate, but you can also figure out for yourself just what it is that you need to do, and everything that'll make you happy. Melanie, you know your mom and I love you, and the last thing we want is for you to hold yourself back because of us," he said.

"I'm not Dad. I swear. I'm just doing this because I know it's what I want in life. I know what I plan to do, and I want to help Alicia too. She's opened up my eyes to many things. She's changed me for the better," she said.

"You really do love her, don't you?"

"Maybe. I don't know, it feels like...it feels like I should've admitted this to myself sooner, but I'm happier. I really am," she admitted.

"Then do what makes you happy Melanie. I knew what that's like. Everyone's telling me to sit down, quit messing with everything, but I'm going to continue this, especially since being with my family makes me happy, and being the best dad I can, is my goal," he said.

"Thanks Dad. You've helped me a lot. I feel good, and I'm interested in potentially making this work with Alicia," she said.

"Well, do what you need to do. Do what you feel is right in your heart. No matter what, I'll always support you," he said to her.

"Thanks Dad. I appreciate it," she said.

Melanie proceeded to show off the paintings to her father and when she got to the last one, she tried to hide it.

"What's that?"

"Oh, it's nothing. Don't worry about it," she said.

"I can see it's quite beautiful," he said.

"I mean, it is," she said.

"Is that for her?" he asked.

She blushed but nodded.

"Yeah, it's for Alicia. It's my Christmas gift," she said.

"She's going to love it," he said. Melanie smiled at those words, feeling encouraged to continue her art, no matter what happened next.

She was happy, and she felt like she could tell her dad was feeling the same way. She then noticed he was smiling, for the first time in forever.

"You're happy with my choice, aren't you Dad?"

"Of course. I'm glad when my daughter makes choices that benefit her, and I'm glad that she could figure it out for herself. But I'm sure this is just the beginning," he said to her.

"It is Dad. It's the beginning of our future," she admitted.

Melanie realized the truth, that she loved Alicia, that this was the perfect gift for her. They would make it, no matter what the odds may be. She was just ready for the future, and no matter what happened.

The next day, Melanie went into work. Brayden was at the counter, ringing up items.

"Is Alicia here yet?"

"Nope. She said she was feeling a little sick, so I told her that she should come in later on," he offered.

"That's fine. It's weird, ever since I took that job at the branch office, things have been a whole lot easier for me here. I don't feel like I'm stuck in a rut or anything," she said.

"Oh yeah, you're going to be working there soon. Are you excited?

"As ready as I'll ever be, if I'm going to be honest," she said.

She didn't know what would happen. She feared what might transpire, but at the same time, she was ready for this new adventure.

"You know, there is something I want to tell you. But I didn't want to come off as weird, since Danny pulled that stunt a little while ago," he said.

"Oh yeah. Him. I'm glad we finally outed him for the weirdo he was. He got so mad because she wasn't into him," Melanie said.

"Yeah. I get that though. I mean, maybe he felt he had a chance. I figured out a long time ago that I didn't have a hell of a chance with you," he said.

"You mean...you liked me?" she said.

"Yeah. Melanie, I've liked you for a long time, but I could tell that you didn't feel the same way. It's not a big deal to me. I mean, we all come to terms with the truth, that not everyone is into us, but I did feel a little sad at first. But I'd rather be a friend to you than someone pining over you when I know I don't have a hell of a chance," he said.

Melanie looked at Braydon.

"You've been a good friend for a long time Braydon. You encouraged me to talk to Alicia," she said.

"Yeah, and I'm glad that I did. Melanie, I started seeing another woman, and I feel so much better. I feel like I can finally get over the past, and look forward to the future," he said.

"You mean it?"

"Damn right I do. I know this was the ass-kicking I needed, and I wouldn't have this any other way," he said.

"Well, I'm glad that you mean that," she said.

'right. Well, I'm happy that you're here, and you seem happier too," he said.

"I do. I'm happier Braydon. I feel like I'm finally making the changes that I want to in life, the ones that I feel are necessary for me," she said.

"Well, you're always welcome to talk to me about anything. No matter what, it'll all be okay," he said to her.

"For sure. Thanks Braydon.

Melanie waited at the store, and finally, after an hour, Alicia came in. he looked like a mess, with her hair tied back, a forlorn look on her face, and annoyance radiating from her.

"Hey Alicia. You okay?"

"I've been better. My mom came home last night. We had another argument. I really can't do this anymore. I want our Melanie, but I'm scared to leave," she said.

"Alicia, you're either going to continue to be miserable, or you do something about this. I suggest the latter. You're better off without her," Melanie said. She was sick of seeing Alicia hurt like this.

"I know this, but that doesn't mean that I'm not concern about what will happen next," she said.

"Well, you've got me. I'll help as best as I can," she said.

Alicia seemed happier about this. After Melanie said those words, Alicia then sighted.

"Thanks Mel. You're right. I am better off. That's why I think this weekend I'm going to leave finally. She doesn't seem to have any work on Sunday, so I'll leave Saturday. I know she'll be around later at night, when I can finally say bye to her. This is for the best really. I can't continue going on like this Melanie. I don't want to," she said.

"Then don't. leave her. Pursue your dreams," she said.

"You're right. I will," Alicia said.

Melanie noticed a chance. Alicia felt more confident the moment she uttered those words. Alicia then went to work, and that night, she told Melanie she'd prepare to move on Saturday. Her mom wouldn't be home till later on, and while Melanie could tell that Alicia was nervous about this, she put her hand on her shoulder, reassuring Alicia that everything would be all right.

It was a scary situation confronting the one person who made their lives miserable and standing up for themselves, but if there's one thing that Melanie's learned recently, it's that taking a chance, being with the person that they love, and focusing on the fact that you love the person rather than the intricacies of the relationship was much better for both of them.

She was happy, and that's ultimately all that mattered at the end of the day.

Chapter Thirteen

Alicia prepared for this. She had a lot to lose, but a whole lot to gain as well. She contacted her dad, just to couple check that it was okay to move everything over, and he laughed once more.

"Of course. I'll be over in the morning with my moving truck if that works," Alicia's father said.

"Thanks, Dad. I appreciate it. Very much so," she said.

Alicia felt nervous about this. She'd been slowly packing everything up, and the night before, she had all but her bed, bedsheets, and clothes for the next day in boxes. Moving out of one's parents' house was supposed to be a sad thing, but for Alicia, it felt riveting.

It felt like she was starting a new life. Alicia felt like she was on top of the hill, but that was when she noticed it.

Her mom was here.

Why the hell was she here? Alicia then went over to the office, opening the door.

"Hey, Mom, what are you doing here?"

"Didn't I tell you not to bother me? I swear Alicia, I think about kicking you out every single day, but you're important for paying rent," she said.

Alicia then looked at her with a gasp.

"So, you're saying I only matter because I pay the rent?" Alicia spat.

"Yes. I'd be so happy if I didn't even have to see you anymore. I swear Alicia, you just want to create trouble for everyone. You're a brat, and I'm tired of this and—"

Suddenly, there was a honk. Alicia's mom looked at Alicia with shock on her face. She then looked at the door.

"Who is that?" she said.

Alicia felt her palms sweat, her body tense as her mother ambled toward the doorway, opening it up. Sure enough, it was her dad, but also Melanie there too.

"Nikki. I didn't expect to see you there," he said.

"Mark, what the hell are you doing here?" she asked.

"I'm here to take Alicia with me. She asked for me to take her in, and I offered to do it," he said.

Alicia's mom looked at her with a glare.

"What the hell makes you think I'll be okay with this?" her mom said.

"Because I'm a legal adult, and I can do what I want. And, thanks for withholding the information about my dad from me. Some parent you are," Alicia spat right back. She was not going to have any of this.

"Well, you don't seem to understand Alicia. You're just jealous," she said.

"I'm jealous? I think that's projection, Mom. I'm going to leave, and I'm going to finally live my own life without someone breathing down my neck every two seconds," she snapped back.

"I'd like to see you try," Nikki said.

"Well, Nikki, you can't legally keep her here. She's not a child anymore. Just like how I don't pay child support. She doesn't have to continue living with you," Mark said.

"Why are you taking her side? Don't you understand I need her here?" she said.

"You don't need anyone, Nicki. You have some growing up to do. Also, good to know that you're still the same as ever, a big mess, someone who can't seem to get her life together, who wants to use others as a way to project their issues onto others. You sicken me, Nicki," Mark replied to her with a scoff.

"Well, at least I didn't go off and marry some random guy after getting divorced," he said.

"My husband is a wonderful human being. Maybe you should take some pointers from the rest of your family. We're all in better relationships. I'm going to be a better father to Alicia than I ever was. Right now, you've lost her," he said.

"But Mark—"

"She doesn't have to associate with you. Alicia is an adult, and she's welcomed to leave as she pleases. Now, if you'll excuse me, I'm going to help my daughter get moved in," he said.

He walked inside, and immediately, Alicia saw Melanie there.

"And who the hell are you?"

"I'm Alicia's girlfriend, Melanie. You probably remember me from high school. You told me that I was a piece of shit and a terrible human being while you were in a drunken rampage," she said.

"I barely remember you. You've been here before. You changed my daughter into this thing," she said.

"I didn't do anything to your daughter, Nikki. She chose for herself. She's allowed to have her own life, her own opinions, and you're legally allowed to ignore all of this," she said.

"I—"

"I'm helping my girlfriend move out to her new place. Step aside," Melanie said to her.

She looked at Melanie with boggled eyes, but quickly scampered out of the way as Melanie went in. Alicia then looked at her mother.

"You're doing this, aren't you?" she said.

"Yes, I am. I'm tired, Mom. I'm tired of you not being a caring parent. You just said a few moments ago you'd be happy if I left. So, I'm doing you a favor, and getting the hell out of here," she said.

Nikki looked at her daughter with surprise.

"Please don't. Not right before Christmas," she said.

"Mom, you ruined your chances with many people. You deserve whatever comes to you," she said.

Alicia walked upstairs, grabbing the boxes and heading on down. Thankfully, there wasn't much, but she saw her mom in the corner, head in her hands, and for a long time, she shrugged. She felt terrible about the way that her mom felt, but at the same time, she didn't want to feel remorse.

"Don't worry about her Alicia. Your mom will learn her lesson. You can let her into your life in the future, but I think for now, she needs to learn that the actions and the way she treats others does have consequences, and it's better if she learns this now, and the hard way, rather than down the line when it's too late," he said.

Alicia looked at her mom. Alicia knew that if she made a chance, she would be willing to let her back into her life. For now, there wasn't a chance she would do that.

Her mom ruined everything before. She was tired of letting that hold her back.

"Bye, Mom. I hope you learn from this," she said.

"I did learn. That you're a lying little shit, just like your father," she spat.

"You can believe what you want. I'm leaving," Alicia said.

Alicia walked on out of there, turning around and looking at her mom once more. It hurt to see her like this, and she felt like there was a lot of thing she could utter to her mom right then and there, but right now, she felt...malice. For the first time in forever, she really did feel malice.

As Alicia sat in the back, she looked at her dad, and at her girlfriend.

"Thank you. Both of you. You two didn't need to help out like this, but the fact that you did is very sweet," Alicia said.

"I'm just tired of your mom thinking that she can continue down this path of hate. I'm trying to help her learn a lesson here," her dad said.

"Yeah, and I just want to see my girlfriend happy," Melanie said.

"Well, I feel much happier now," Alicia replied.

"By the way, Melanie, you're more than welcomed to come to Christmas with my husband and Alicia. You're part of our family now. You've helped my daughter get out of a terrible situation, and for that, I thank you," he said.

"You're welcomed, Mark. I'm happy to be a part of the family," she said.

The three of them got back to the apartment in just a few moments. Alicia felt happy when she walked inside. Her dad showed her the bedroom that she had, which was off the main hallway. Her dad was in a whole different area, giving her a sense of privacy, which was perfect.

Most of all, Alicia didn't feel alone anymore. She didn't feel like she just stuck around there because she had nowhere else to go. Instead, she felt happy, and she felt ready for whatever the future would bring at her.

That night, Alicia let Melanie stay over. The two of them lay in bed together, and Alicia looked at Melanie with a smile.

"Thank you for everything, Melanie. You've helped me realize I's okay to be the person you want to be, to not be the victim of abuse anymore," she said.

"I know Alicia. I'm glad that I am here for you. I'm always going to stay by your side," Melanie replied, giving Alicia a kiss on the lips. They sat there, kissing and savoring the feeling of each other, happy and satisfied.

This was a Christmas gift that made Alicia smile, and it was one that she wouldn't forget, even if the world ended, and things never changed.

Chapter Fourteen

It was an understatement that Melanie was happy in fact, she felt like she was a whole new person walking into the branch office the Monday after getting Alicia settled in, signing all of the paperwork to get the ob. The person in charge looked at Melanie, smiling.

"You seem happy to start," they pointed out.

"I'm just happy that everything's falling into place, that I don't feel like I'm hiding anything anymore," she said.

"Well, that's good. You're going to be a valuable part of the team, so we're delighted to have you," she said.

"Thanks. I'm happy to be here," she said.

Alicia seemed to be doing the same thing. Melanie got a call the next day from Alicia on the break.

"Hey there," Alicia said.

"Hi. So, what's up?" Melanie asked.

"Well, I went in to sign the paperwork for the animation company. It's literally everything I expected. They will give me my own desk. I'll be working alone, and they're already giving me my first paid project, I just have to track the time whenever I work on it. I'm so excited I could scream Melanie," she said.

"Good. Scream about it. I'm happy for you. The job at the branch office is shaping up to be good for us too. The other coworkers heard about you, and they don't care. It's nice being in a place where people understand that this is not a bad thing, that it's okay to have a partner of the same gender. I feel much more liberated than I did at the store," she said.

"I do too. I liked working with you, but it's best if we stop doing that, especially if we want to maintain a professional appearance in the office," Alicia pointed out.

"You know, that's a great point. Anyway, my family is having Christmas dinner on Christmas eve. If you want, we can go there and then your dad's in the morning," she said.

"You sure?" Alicia said.

"Of course. My family is very excited to meet you," Melanie said.

"I'm excited too. Do you want to stay over there, or at my place?"

"I actually would prefer your place. My place is going to be filled with people. I'd prefer to give you the present I have in private if that's okay," she said.

"I was thinking the same thing. Plus, I'd rather not get some comments from family about playing phone games and stuff," Alicia said.

Melanie laughed.

"Well, you shouldn't do it at dinner, but I feel that. yeah, my parents are all about everyone getting involved, and I understand if that isn't your style," Melanie replied. She knew her family wouldn't leave them alone if they did stay over there.

"But yeah, I'm down if you are," she said.

"I am too."

Melanie clicked the phone off, feeling happy that everything is shaping up to be perfect, especially right before Christmas.

On Christmas eve, Melanie got home a little early to get dressed. Alicia said she'd be over in a little bit; she was getting ready and getting the house properly taken care of. Then, about an hour later, Alicia rang the doorbell. Melanie heard it, racing over to get the door before her parents did.

"Hey there!" Melanie said.

"Hey! Merry Christmas," Alicia said.

They hugged, and Melanie gave her a kiss on the cheek. They walked inside, seeing Melanie's family there.

It wasn't just the immediate family but extended too. Most of them looked at Alicia with curiosity. Most of them probably thought Alicia was just a friend.

"Hey there. Alicia, you might remember my mom from high school. Mom, this is Alicia," Melanie said.

"Hello dear. You've grown up," Melanie's mom said.

"Yeah, I mean, we're both adults now."

"And in a relationship," she said.

Melanie blushed. She hoped nobody would get offended by that.

"Yes, Mom, we're together," Melanie said.

"Is this your girl?" a man said.

Melanie looked up, seeing her dad there with an eager grin on his face, extending his hand.

"Dad, this is Alicia, my girlfriend. You probably don't remember her because you were working a lot when she was around. Now you get to meet each other," she said.

"Indeed. I'm very excited to meet you. I'm Ralph," he said.

"Hello, sir. It's a pleasure to be here," Alicia said.

The other family members greeted them, and Melanie could feel the tension in her body. She feared what might transpire from this, mostly because she knew that some of her extended family didn't know much about people who were gay. But they all were friendly. Melanie breathed a sigh of relief.

Christmas dinner was how it usually was, and that was both awkward, but also wholesome. Her dad was talking to Alicia about his job, since he liked to do investments, and Alicia was listening. Melanie's mom smiled, and Melanie blushed as she looked at Alicia smiling. Melanie's mom whispered into her ear.

"She seems so happy," she said.

"She doesn't get to have Christmases like this," Melanie admitted.

"Well tell her once you're done here that she's welcome here whenever she wants," her mother said.

Melanie smiled. She was glad her family liked her so much. Melanie feared that it might be weird because Alicia was a girl, but they all accepted it, like it was nothing.

After dinner, they went under the Christmas tree.

"By the way, I'm giving Alicia her present later. We wanted to do something private together," she said.

"Of course. I mean, you two need to have your Christmas together too," her mother said.

"Yeah, plus I know what she got you already. You're going to love it," she said.

Alicia flushed, and Melanie coughed.

"Anyway, let's do this," she said.

She felt so nervous, but everyone liked their gifts. Melanie got her parents a little gift card to eat at a restaurant, and they got her some new art supplies.

"Wow, you guys listened," she said.

"We wanted to make sure that you got what you wanted. We don't fully understand, but we are going to try our best to be supportive. Plus, you want to keep it as a hobby, correct?" he said.

"Of course. That's the plan," Melanie said.

They all spent time around the tree, talking and having a great time. When it was about nine, Melanie got up, taking Alicia's hand.

"I'll be back tomorrow, but I'm spending the night at Alicia's. Merry Christmas!" Melanie cried out.

The family all said their goodbyes as they made their way to Alicia's place of Christmas. There was a silence, and Alicia seemed nervous.

"Is everything okay?" Melanie asked.

"Yeah, I'm just nervous. I have something for you, but I'd prefer if we did presents tomorrow night. I want you to spend time with my dad and his husband first. Then, tomorrow we can do it. I'm just so happy I have a normal Christmas for the first time ever. It's really exciting to do this. Thanks, Melanie," she said.

"Are you sure about that? I mean, it'll be a little bit of time before I can give you your gift then," she said.

"It's all right. There's something big that I want to give to you, and I'm a bit nervous about it. Plus, it's good because my dad said he was going with Bruce to see a movie and walk through and see the lights tomorrow. So, we'll get a little more privacy," Alicia said.

"Fine by me. Works for me," she said.

They got back, and Melanie and Alicia had their Christmas unwrapping at Alicia's house. Her dad and Bruce spied them, getting them gift cards, and a slew of other gifts. Alicia didn't know what to do other than to look at them. Melanie laughed.

"You don't have to look at it like a deer in headlights," she said.

"This is the nicest Christmas I've experienced in a long time," she said.

"It's been a wonderful time. I'm glad that we could do this," she said.

"I glad as well," she replied.

Melanie felt happy and satisfied, reassured that she was doing the right thing with Alicia. She didn't feel like she was scared anymore, but instead, ready for the future with her girlfriend. Tomorrow, they'd give their presents and celebrate Christmas dinner, and Melanie knew for a fact that it would be magical.

This Christmas would change everything. Melanie was okay with the changes. It meant that she would get to make another person happy. It was someone who she loved more than anything else in the world, and someone who Melanie wanted to see be successful in the long haul.

Chapter Fifteen

Alicia felt like this was the start of a new, more significant change beginning to form, and when they got to her new home, she felt smitten.

"It's so weird this is all happening like this. I'm happy though," she said.

"What do you mean?" Melanie said.

"You know, with the way our relationship turned out, our new life, my dad being happier than he was before, it's nice, that's all," she said.

"I feel this so much. I'm happy too. I wasn't sure if things would work out the way that they have, but they are. It's a bit refreshing, if I'm going to be honest with you," she said.

"I know. It's refreshing to me as well," she replied.

When they got inside, they saw her dad and Bruce sitting in the living room.

"There you two are. We were thinking Christmas presents tomorrow," he said.

"Fine with me," Melanie said to him.

"Yeah Dad, I'm just here to have a nice time with you. I don't really care what happens tonight," she said.

"Well, I guess we can sit around the Christmas tree and watch some movies and such. I was thinking a nice Christmas breakfast tomorrow," he said.

"Yeah, that's fine with me," Melanie said.

"Same here," Alicia replied.

"Anyway, I'll be down here. When you two are ready, you just let me know," he said.

Melanie and Alicia both nodded, heading upstairs to put their stuff down. It was so different to be spending Christmas like this. That night, it was mostly spent watching Christmas movies and having a good time. However, at midnight, Alicia's dad looked at her. Alicia was confused. What did he want to do?

"I was thinking we could try a new, different tradition, if that's cool with you," he said.

"Sure Dad. What is it?" Alicia asked.

"I was thinking that, if you're interested, we could open up presents tonight. Again though, that's up to you," he said.

Alicia and Melanie looked at each other.

"We can do this with you tonight, but Alicia wants to do ours tomorrow," Melanie said.

"Yeah sure. That's totally fine," he said.

"Good," Melanie said.

"Yeah, I would like to do ours separately. I know that we have our own little things to give to each other," Alicia admitted.

"Well, that's fine here," he said to them.

Melanie looked at Alicia, and it was evident that she had a few things to say to her. Alicia definitely felt nervous as ever about everything that's there, and she wondered if there was anything that could quell the nerves, but she didn't think so. As they sat around under the tree, Alicia's father gave Alicia a variety of gifts. He did the same for Melanie, and when they looked at him with surprise, he simply smiled.

"This is for both of you, since you two are a part of my life now, and I want you both to be happy," he said.

"Thank you, Dad," Alicia said.

She unwrapped the gifts, finding a new animation tablet, and a new laptop and keyboard and mouse system. A look of surprise blossomed her face as she did this.

"Whoa, are you serious Dad?" she asked.

"Of course. This is for you. I want to see you do well with your new job. I'm sure you've been working on an old-ass laptop for a long time, and I don't think you need that for what you're about to do," he said to Alicia. Alicia listened to him, and she then nodded.

"I know, Dad. I have been...but how did you...think of this?" she said.

"I only want what's best for my daughter. I know you've got a lot going on Alicia, and I want to be the best and most helpful father that I can," he said.

Alicia smiled, feeling excited about everything, and feeling like this was indeed the beginning of it all. She didn't feel like she was being tossed to the side anymore, but instead, Alicia felt like she was finally included in everything that was happening.

"Dad, you don't know how much this means to me," she said.

"I do, Alicia. I understand all of the trouble you have going on, all of the struggles you're feeling. I know how it is, and I know how you're always struggling with the way things are. I think it's safe to say that you need someone special, someone who can be there for you no matter what, and someone who will help you. I want to be a better parent to you than I was before. Because I'm here now, and I'm not leaving anytime soon," he said.

Alicia listened to this, surprised by everything that was transpiring. She felt like she was finally accepted for who she was.

"Thank you so much, Dad. Seriously this is wonderful," she said.

"I only want what's best for you, Alicia. I know that it's not easy for you, but hopefully, even with all that's going on, you get the best results from your efforts, and together, we make it the best life that we can. I'll always be here for you, and I'm sure that Melanie will be the emotional and physical support you need too," he said.

Alicia turned to Melanie, who smiled at her.

"Damn right I will be," Melanie said.

Alicia felt excited about everything, ready to take on the future. Her new job, her new life with Melanie, all of this would work out swimmingly.

"And, I will say that whenever you two are ready to finally get up and leave, you guys can. I understand that both of you are grown adults. I hope we continue to have a healthy relationship even after you two leave me," he said.

"Yeah, we can," Alicia said. She wasn't going to abandon her father, and she felt like he was definitely the best person to have around with all that was happening.

"If you ever need anything, Mark, don't hesitate to ask," Melanie said.

"Thank you, Melanie. But right now, I just want to see my daughter happy. I've been a bit of a mess since I was out of the family for so long, and now, now that I'm here again, now that I'm able to have a normal life with both of you, I want to make sure that the actions I take are meaningful," he said.

"They are. Thanks, Dad," Alicia said.

"Indeed. Not everyone can say they have a supportive parent like you. I love my family, but I'm also happy knowing that Alicia has the support that she has, too," Melanie said.

"Indeed. She's had a rough time with her mother. I'm very sorry for leaving you with that woman Alicia. I'm serious. If I knew half the stuff she was doing, she wouldn't have taken you. I would've figured out a way to make sure I got custody of you, somehow, some way," he said.

"It's cool, Dad. I didn't expect it either," she said.

"I know, but still. It's not something I'm particularly happy about," he said.

He did feel regret, and Alicia nodded.

"It's not your fault, Dad. It's not like you could've predicted her actions," she said.

"That's true. Your mother is a short fuse in her own way. But we're working through it. She needs some time to herself, and some time away from you to realize her faults, I think. That's just the way things are with your mom Alicia. She's a good woman deep down, but also someone that I feel will need to learn all her lessons the hard way," he said.

"Yeah, she's going to have to," Alicia admitted. She knew her mom wasn't the best at learning any of these either. But it was better if she did this all on her own.

"Anyway, let's continue unwrapping gifts and such," he said.

The group sat down, each of them unwrapping gifts, ignoring the conversation that they had up till now. Alicia felt like she was experiencing a real family gathering. It wasn't just her with a parent because she had to be with them, but she felt like they were actually here for her, no matter what the odds may be. Everything felt a bit surprising. Alicia did like the company of her dad, and with Melanie too.

After they finished their gifts, they all said goodnight to each other. Alicia's dad, however, stopped for a second.

"Alicia, come here," he said.

Alicia did so. Then, she was enveloped in a hug.

"Dad what are you—"

"I'm giving you a hug. Thank you. For everything," he said.

Alicia then looked at him, feeling a bit surprised by everything at hand, realizing that this was the first time he actually hugged her like this. He then pulled away, smiling.

"Bruce and I are leaving for our little getaway in the morning. So, you two can have your own celebration," he said with a wink.

Alicia nodded.

"Thanks, Dad. I appreciate it," she said.

"I know what it's like. I was young at a point too. I know you have a lot you want to say to her, but you're afraid to do it in front of others. It's all good," he said.

"Thank you," she replied.

When they parted ways, Alicia then headed up the stairs to where Melanie was. When they got to the room, Melanie laid down on the bed.

"This is nice," she said.

"Right? My dad is definitely a great guy," she said.

"Indeed. So, what did he need to say to you?"

"He's giving us free access to the house. They're leaving for some little getaway they're having together, so they gave us the run of the place," Alicia said.

"How about in the morning I give you your gift then," Melanie said.

"That's fine. I was thinking the same thing for you," Alicia said.

They said goodnight to each other, happy and satisfied by the way the night went. But Alicia could tell Melanie had something big planned for them, something that she couldn't figure out. She wondered what it was, and if this would change their life. She had a feeling that whatever Melanie had planned, it would be a good time, and they'd enjoy it.

At least, that was what she thought.

Chapter Sixteen

Melanie was nervous.

She didn't know how to convey her nervousness. She just wanted to tell Alicia everything and show her what she gave her, but she also didn't want to come off as a bit weird about it. But it seemed like Alicia was definitely excited to get up the next morning. When they did, Alicia turned to Melanie, giving her a kiss on the lips.

"Thanks. Merry Christmas," she said.

"Thanks, for what?" Melanie asked.

"For being there for me and all. I definitely appreciate it," Alicia said.

"Yeah, I'm glad that you're here with me too. I'm so happy to have you by my side," Melanie said to Alicia.

"I am too. Merry Christmas. I'm excited to give you your gift," she said.

"Oh, I am too," Melanie said.

Alicia got up, starting the coffee, and Melanie lugged her gift to the tree. There was a small little item underneath the tree, and Melanie was confused. It couldn't be a ring, could it?

Melanie didn't believe so, but she wouldn't put it past her to get that. As they sat down, the tension in the air was so thick you could cut it with a knife. Melanie then heard Alicia speak.

"By the way, my present isn't an engagement ring. I'm not ready for that, and neither are you. I want to get married eventually, but I think right now, we need to take some time to really get our lives together before any of that," she said.

"That's fine. I think that'll be okay," Melanie said.

"Anyway, I guess we should start this," she said.

"Yeah. We should," Melanie said.

The two of them simply sat. For a moment, Melanie didn't say anything. She then gave Alicia the gift, blushing.

"This is for you. I hope you like it," she said.

Melanie looked at Alicia, who took the present, holding it there.

"All right," she said.

She opened up the gift, and when she pulled it out, her jaw dropped.

"No way," she said.

"It's not bad, right?"

"Not at all! I'm just surprised, that's all. I mean, you made this, didn't you?" she said.

"Yes, I did. I made it myself. The thing is, my parents talked it over with me, and I think they're okay with me going through with a small art career on the side. They just don't want it to be a big thing for me right now. they don't want me to only focus on that," she said.

"No, that makes complete sense. I'm surprised really," she said.

"Yeah. I am too," Melanie said.

The two of them flushed, looking at each other, trying to figure out how to really talk about this.

"Anyway, you think we can...maybe get to my gift?" she said, grinning.

"Yeah, here," Alicia said.

Melanie looked at the gift. It was so small that she had no idea what it was. But then, when she opened it, she noticed it was a flash drive.

"What is this?" she said.

"Here, let me get my laptop. I wanted to give you something a little more sentimental than usual, I just hope it isn't lame or anything," Alicia said.

"I don't think it's lame," Melanie said.

Alicia plugged it in, turning it on, and what Melanie saw almost made her burst into tears. She sat there, tears in her eyes, and she looked at her with surprise in her eyes.

"This is beautiful," she said.

It was a video of the two of them, the memories they shared together, both in high school and beyond. It was a whole little video documenting their life. As Melanie watched it, she saw at the end their future.

The two of them walking down the aisle, holding hands and marrying each other. The future that they've always dreamed of. The one she gets to share with Alicia if they continue being in a relationship.

"You really want that?" she said.

"Of course, Melanie. I'm so happy that you're here with me, and I don't want to lose you," she said.

"I really don't either. You make me feel happy, my heart whole, and I'm just so surprised really," she said.

"Yeah, I'm surprised too, but I'm definitely excited for our future," she said.

"I am too, Melanie. I really am. I feel like, no matter what, it'll all be okay," she said.

"Yeah, it'll definitely be okay," she said to Alicia. Melanie had a good feeling about their future. The two of them leaned forward, giving each other a long, passionate kiss.

"I am very excited to start my new job at the beginning of the year," Alicia said.

"You and me both. And, I mean, my parents are pretty cool with me continuing my art on the side. I'm making some decent cash off it, so it's working out for me," she said to Alicia.

"That's amazing! I'm excited," Alicia replied.

"I'm excited to finally get started on my future. I know things haven't been easy for us. But sometimes, you just need to deal with things in order to have a better outcome. It's important to realize sometimes you need to sift through the crap in order for it to get better," he said.

Alicia agreed with those words, and Melanie could see the smile on her face.

"You know, I was also thinking that we could work together to help you set up your shop too. Since I know that, once you have that together, you can take on new orders. I think my graphic design skills could be of use here," Alicia offered.

Melanie immediately nodded.

"I would love that," she said.

"I would love that too," she replied.

Melanie felt revitalized on relationships. In the past, most of the time it was just some guys who only cared about her for her body, or just wanted to get in her pants. But to have someone so loving, so caring, and who only wanted what's best for her, is something that made Melanie realize that things were better than before, and they made it work.

"Thank you for everything Melanie. I do appreciate it," Alicia said.

"No, thank you. You made things better for both of us," she said.

"I think it's a mutual thing. Mostly because, I know that no matter what, we'd be okay," she said.

"I know that feeling. I definitely am happy with the results of this, she replied.

They then stayed there, looking at each other for a second. Melanie felt happy, mostly because she was with the woman that she loved. But then, Alicia tensed, and Melanie looked at her with concern.

"I sometimes wonder what the future holds. I'm a little scared. like...will this job be perfect for us, or will it end up in failure?" she said.

"Well, the answer to that is simple: if you think it'll end in failure, chances are, it probably will," Melanie said.

"You're right. That's obvious," she said.

"The best thing to do at this point, Alicia, is to figure out what to do from here. We can plan our entire future later on. It's Christmas. Today, we can do what makes the both of us happy. And that's something I think you'll love," Melanie purred.

Alicia immediately knew what it was. She then looked at Melanie, leaning in, and capturing her lips with Melanie's. Melanie then pulled her close, deepening the kiss at this point. Both of them felt happy, and for Melanie, she knew that, no matter what happened next, everything would be okay. Alicia was with her, and Alicia seemed happy, so she didn't want to let this go.

It was the beginning of their new life, their future, and Melanie was determined to give this Christmas present to Alicia today, and make her feel good.

But, little did she know that Alicia had her own little gift, something different from the norm, and ready to be experienced by both.

Chapter Seventeen

Alicia kissed Melanie with a flurry of passion that wasn't there before. She kept their lips together, their lips meshing and teasing each other with a riot of motion. She heard Melanie start to moan as she did this, and Alicia felt a smile ghost her lips as this happened.

The two of them continued to explore each other for a while, kissing and teasing, when Alicia moved, sitting in Melanie's lap and grinning at her.

"What are you—"

"I'm in charge right now, Melanie. I want to make you feel great, and I'm going to make you happy," she said.

That was the one gift that Melanie hadn't gotten either of them. Alicia was going to take the first step and provide the first move. Melanie looked at Alicia, and for a second, she blushed.

"So, you're in charge tonight," she said.

"That I am. You ready?"

"Oh yes. I'm very much ready," Melanie said.

Alicia smiled, pushing her lips against Melanie's, and Alicia took control. She pushed her tongue in, letting their muscles move and interact with each other in a passionate moment that only they would know. Alicia felt a bit of satisfaction when she heard Melanie let out a small, subtle cry.

She knew her dad and Bruce wouldn't be back for a while. It was their own vacation, and Melanie and Alicia knew that this little bit of privacy was something that they should take advantage of. Alicia knew her dad wouldn't be too in their face, not like her mom whenever she was around, but for now, she didn't want to worry about it. They shared a tender, sensual romance, and a kiss that made them both excited for so much more.

But tonight, Melanie was hers, and she was going to tease and pleasure her in ways she wasn't used to. She wanted to see Melanie squirm, and it was something that she craved more than anything else.

As she did this, her hands moved toward Melanie's robe, undoing it to reveal the small, lacy underwear that she had on underneath.

"Was this planned?" Alicia asked.

"Maybe. Maybe I wanted to see if you'd do something about this," Melanie purred with arousal.

Alicia blushed, but she liked the sound of this. She knew that Melanie was aroused and she could see the small hint of nipple poking on out from the confines of the bra. She let her fingers drift downward till she got to those nipples, pushing them and teasing them slightly.

As she did that, she noticed Melanie immediately tense up, her breath hitching for but a moment as she started to let her hands dangle and tease against the flesh there. She watched with rapt delight as Melanie grasped the arms of the couch, letting out a small series of gasps and moans with every single motion. It was perfect, totally perfect, and for Alicia, she felt like she was doing the one thing that she knew Melanie would love, and of course enjoy.

She moved toward the bra, pulling it off to the side, revealing her pinkened bud. She clutched her lips onto this, kissing it with subtle touches while her other hand teased the other nipple without hesitation. Melanie let out a small gasp, as she began to tease and feel the effects of this. Alicia could see her coming undone, and tonight, she would take care of Melanie.

This was the woman that changed her life. The person she always felt like was a part of her life more than she cared to admit. She was also the woman who made her realize the essence of her sensuality, so it would only make sense to have all of this happen. She quickly moved toward the edge of the other nipple, flicking her tongue against there, causing a sudden gasp and moan to elicit from Melanie.

This was perfect. The perfect moment, and Alicia was enjoying every single minute of this.

She continued to tease, touch, and pleasure Melanie's nipples, feeling the rapt delight with every single sound that came out of her mouth. It was so perfect, the pleasure of the moment so obvious, and as Alicia watched her start to slowly come undone, it was all making her feel excitement that she didn't expect to feel. She loved that Melanie was coming undone right in front of her, and the feeling of control was enough to tease and entice her even more. "You want me to continue?" she asked after she licked a trail up to Melanie's neck, nibbling on the flesh there.

"Y-yes," she said.

She was in control of Melanie tonight. She knew that Melanie was enjoying everything about this. As Alicia gave Melanie a soft, sensual kiss, she moved her lips downward, moving toward the distinct pinkened area below.

She had on a pair of sheer pink panties that showed off everything. Her hands moved toward Melanie's slit, touching and teasing. The sounds that came from Melanie were the perfect harmony, the sounds that made her shudder with delight at the sensation of this, and when she did tease Melanie, watching her start to moan and cry out like this, Alicia wondered how she got so damn lucky. She never got to see this here, but here she was, watching as Melanie started to grasp the arms of the couch, crying out with widened eyes at the sensations that were there.

Alicia was relentless though, pumping her with her fingers, watching Melanie's eyes dilate like that, it was all so perfect, the heat of the sensual moment.

She then moved between Melanie's legs, kissing up her inner thigh until she got to the labia of where Melanie's slit was, looking at it, smelling her essence for a second, and then, gripping the sides of her panties as she slid them downward.

Melanie flushed crimson as Alicia want to work on her, touching, kissing, and teasing every which way. Everything about this was perfect, and everything that she did with Melanie was something that she wanted. Melanie was already crying out in pure, utter pleasure. Alicia knew that Melanie was getting closer and closer with every single possible moment. She then let her tongue slide against Melanie's sweet spot, touching and teasing her. When it finally caresses against the one area that made Melanie crazy, she then screamed out, lifting her legs, and then, she had her orgasm.

Alicia got the full taste of it, lapping it up, savoring it with every possible moment at hand. She looked at Melanie with a grin on her face.

"You good love?" she said.

"Yeah. Wonderful actually. But I also have something that you probably would like too," Melanie said with a purr.

"Oh? What is it?" she asked.

Melanie gave her a grin, and Alicia knew it was something she'd like. Suddenly, Melanie grabbed a vibrator from behind her, but it had two heads on each side.

"Wait is this—"

"Yeah, with the extra money I'm making with this new gig, I figured I'd get something that we'd both enjoy," she said.

"Wow, this is amazing," she said.

"I know. I'm so excited to use this," she said to Alicia.

Alicia then nodded.

"I am too," she said.

The two of them kissed as Alicia inserted it into Melanie. She let out a small cry as it fully settled itself. Alicia did the same thing, pushing it inside, and then, when she turned it on, she suddenly felt her body tense up.

"Oh my God!" she said.

Alicia then started to let out a series of cries, and so did Melanie. Alicia felt like all of her sensations that she was feeling were heightened to the next level, creating a level of arousal that even she wasn't ready for. Melanie did the same thing, holding her there as they moved together, feeling the pleasure, the waxing moments, and the arousal of this. It was like the perfect Christmas gift for them, and Alicia was definitely in a whole new world with it.

The two of them kissed, touched, and moaned each other's name. They were aroused and turned on by the sheer nature of their lovemaking. They held each other and kissed with a passion that neither of them expected.

The first to orgasm was, of course, Melanie. She was already pretty spent, and when she finally did, Alicia held her there, kissing her with a wrought-iron passion that they both enjoyed. Alicia did the same thing, grasping her body, moving back and forth, and for Alicia, when it happened, she threw her head back, crying out loud.

"Ahh!" Alicia said, feeling her entire body tense for but a moment, and then relax shortly after.

It was the best feeling, the most amazing moment, and for Alicia, she didn't know what to do, other than to sit there, bask in the afterglow of her orgasm, and enjoy everything about it. For a second, she didn't say anything, and neither did Melanie.

"Are you doing okay?" she said.

"Yeah, I'm wonderful. What about you?" Alicia said.

"Oh, I'm great. Just, wow," Melanie said with a smile on her face. Alicia laughed at it, and for moment, neither of them didn't need to say a word.

They'd been through a lot, and with all of these new changes, it was no wonder they were so tense. It was like they needed this, both enjoying the sensation and loving every moment of the journey at hand. The sensation, the fun that they experienced, and the results that they both got out of this, was enough to make them enjoy the moment and the pleasure of it all.

They lay back, smiling at each other, and there was an air of happiness on both of their faces. Neither of them was upset, and neither of them had any doubts. Right now, the moment was all about them, and that's what made it worth it.

"Hey, Melanie?" Alicia asked.

"What's up?"

"Do you think we can continue to have Christmases like this?" she asked.

Alicia didn't want this to be the end. But then, Melanie moved in, giving her a long, drawn-out kiss that said everything. She pulled back, smiling.

"Yeah. My wish is for another Christmas like this, especially in the future," she said.

Alicia beamed, realizing that Melanie was in it for the long haul. She then nodded, grinning.

"Good. Because I am too," Alicia said.

They both shared a long kiss together, neither of them holding back in that moment. Together, they could experience this, and they'd love every moment of this. Alicia and Melanie both knew this, and Alicia knew for a fact that the future was brighter, and she would be happier.

Alicia did wonder if one day she would get to tell her mom everything, and she'd get an apology from her? She doubted it, but she didn't even know anymore. It was something that made her wonder this. But, after a second, Melanie looked at her, giving her a winning smile.

"Your mom would be proud to know that you're doing okay. She doesn't realize it yet, but I think she's going to regret everything, and she'll realize just how much she hurt you," Melanie said.

"Yeah, but this is also the first Christmas without her. Which I mean, I don't really think it's necessarily a bad thing that I decided this, but also feel like it's better this way. I don't want to live a life with her putting me down, and I don't want to experience that anymore," she said.

"Good. You don't have to Alicia. You're strong," Melanie said.

Alicia did know that she was strong. She was happy, and she felt like everything would be okay. Even if things went to hell and back, she'd be happy, and she'd be much better off than where she was beforehand. It was the one thing that she wanted more than anything else, and the one thing that she desired. For Alicia, it was definitely the start of a new life, a new beginning, and a new existence for her, both right now, and of course in the future.

And Alicia knew that there was definitely a lot going for her now. she wasn't under the influence of her mother, she was able to have a successful job, and she had a partner who made her happy. She knew all of this, and while it was sad to know that she didn't have the support of her mom, she realized shortly after that she didn't really have the full support of her, and in general, she was only using Alicia for her own gain.

That's when Alicia realized the truth, that she was better off without her mom in place.

"Melanie?" Alicia asked.

"What's up?" Melanie replied.

"Thank you. For everything," Alicia admitted.

Melanie planted a kiss on Alicia's lips, pulling back and grinning.

"You're very welcome, Alicia. This is the start of a new life for both of us. I'm nervous too. But, we have each other, and we have the support of others, so naturally, I think it'll all be okay," she said.

"Yeah, it will be. I'm sure of it," Alicia said.

That's when everything changed. Alicia stopped worrying about her mother. She did feel guilty that she couldn't be the one to help her, but she also knew that her mom was someone that was past reckoning in a sense. She wasn't just doing this to get away from her mother though. She was doing this as well to be with the person that she loved.

For Alicia, the new job was the best thing for her. She got to work with animators that she only dreamed of working with, people she'd heard of, but never actually got a chance to speak to. It changed her for the better, and for Alicia, she felt like no matter what transpired next, everything would be okay.

Epilogue

After about a year or so, Alicia was promoted to one of the head animators of the studio, and she got to work on her first full-length movie. Melanie was with her every step of the way. She even encouraged Alicia to go through with the job.

As for Melanie, Alicia noticed a change in her too. She took the job with the branch office. Later on, she found she could work in administration for local artists in the area. Melanie decided to do that, using all of the administrative stuff that she already knew. But she was happier because it meant she could work with people that she wanted to, build those connections. After about a year, Melanie was making enough money to leave the current gig she was at, and pursue a career in art.

While Melanie's family didn't like it, Alicia knew that if she supported Melanie, she'd be able to do whatever she needed. Melanie would be supportive of her as well, and they'd have their lives together, no matter what. It was a nice feeling. For Alicia, she was ready to take on the world and build a future.

They did a lot. One day, Alicia got a text message from her mom. It didn't say much, but only a few words.

Hey there. I'm sorry for everything. I'm proud of you. Call me if you want to.

Alicia didn't call her back. For now, she didn't want her mom's toxic ideas around. She felt better just living her own life. While there was a lot that happened, she wished she could tell her mom. Alicia wished it would all be the same. However, it was better just living the life that she had.

Both she and Melanie managed to move out of their parent's homes after a bit. It was easy for Alicia, but for Melanie it was hard. Her dad wasn't doing so great. But he encouraged her to go.

"Go do something with your life," he said.

Alicia and Melanie built the future that they ended up sharing together, and while it did contain some rocky moments, they didn't regret anything they did.

Printed in Great Britain
by Amazon